THE BLACKSTONE DRAGON HEIR

BLACKSTONE MOUNTAIN BOOK 1

ALICIA MONTGOMERY

ALSO BY ALICIA MONTGOMERY

THE TRUE MATES SERIES

Fated Mates

Blood Moon

Romancing the Alpha

Witch's Mate

Taming the Beast

Tempted by the Wolf

THE LONE WOLF DEFENDERS SERIES

Killian's Secret

Loving Quinn

All for Connor

PROLOGUE

She had to stay quiet.

Everyone knew shifters had keen senses. Hearing. Sight. Taste. Smell. She'd taken off her shoes a while back, hoping it would silence her feet on the pavement as she ran. She was wearing dark clothing and it was evening, but that wouldn't do anything since they could see in the dark. Taste, she didn't have to worry about, but smell was another problem. They'd probably gotten a sniff of her in the apartment and were now hunting her down.

This is going to suck, Catherine thought. But she didn't have a choice. Good thing she knew about this alleyway behind a group of restaurants in the strip mall not far from her Los Angeles apartment. Four industrial-sized dumpsters were sitting in front of her. *Eenie, meenie, miney ... who the fuck cared? Just pick one!*

Catherine approached the middle dumpster. The choice was easy because that one had been left open. Gingerly, she grabbed the top and hoisted herself up. She swung a leg over, and her foot caught on the inside edge of the dumpster. *Thank*

God. One more push and she went tumbling over, landing in a wet, slimy pile of steaming food garbage.

She wanted to gag, but she couldn't. Her life depended on her being able to stay quiet. She stood up, got one last gulp of air, then shut the lid. Pinching her nose, she began to breathe through her mouth, which wasn't much better, but she didn't have a choice. Tears pricked at her eyes.

Rissa. Her roommate. Her friend. She was gone. *Those bastards!*

Catherine bit her lip, trying to stop herself from crying out. She knew Rissa had been in a lot of trouble, but she didn't know how deep it went. She was a wild child, loved walking on the dark side, and had a weakness for bad boys.

Goddamn Ivan. She knew he was trouble the moment he walked up to them at the bar where both she and Rissa worked. Catherine knew exactly *what* he was. A shifter. But Rissa was drawn to him like a moth to a flame. And just like said moth, Rissa was gone. Extinguished. Just like that.

"Her scent is here!" The heavily-accented English was distinct in the quiet of the night. It was followed by footsteps echoing throughout the alley.

Fuck. Her body tensed.

"Goddamn garbage!" another voice said. "Can't smell a fucking thing in here. How can you be sure?"

"Her scent ended right outside here. Where would she be?"

"Search everywhere!"

This was it. The end. They would find her, and they would kill her. Put a gun to her head and end her life. Just like they did to Rissa. The moment was frozen in her mind.

The footsteps got closer and closer.

"Come out, come out," one of them mocked. "If you're in here, come out now. I promise it won't hurt. I'll make it quick."

The voice made her blood freeze. He'd been the man who was holding the gun. *Andrei?* That's the name she thought she'd heard.

Her mind was telling her to just give up. It was hopeless. *Don't make them angry.* But, no, she wanted to fight. She didn't come halfway across the world, leaving everything behind, just to be killed. *Fight, damn you!*

Suddenly, a new voice broke the silence in the air. "Who the hell are you and what are you doing?"

"Go back inside," one of the thugs said. "This does not concern you."

"Fuck you. I know you guys. You're from the Chesnovak Brotherhood."

"Yeah, and if you know what's good for you—"

"Oh yeah? Well, my cousin's Giorgio Diviani. Know the name?" Pause. "Yeah, I thought so. The Divianis kicked your asses during the last war. And now we gotta keep the truce, unless we want cops sniffing around or those anti-shifter groups after us again."

"We're looking for someone."

"What the fuck do you think I am? Missing Persons? Get out of here, or I'll call my cousin."

Catherine's heart thumped against her chest as the silence seemed to stretch on.

"Fine. We'll leave."

"And I don't want none of you hanging around. I'll have some of my boys escort you to your car."

The conversation outside became unintelligible as she heard the shuffling of footsteps get farther and farther away from her hiding place.

Catherine sat inside, counting to a hundred before she finally thought it was safe. Opening the top, she took a gulp of the cool air—not fresh, but better than what was inside. She climbed out of the dumpster and ignored the pain that shot through her ankle as her bare feet connected with the ground.

Shit, shit, shit. Too close. But it wasn't over. Those guys were going to hunt her down and kill her. Fuck. She had to get out of town. L.A. had been her home for a year, but she didn't really feel connected here. It was just a place to pass through until she figured things out.

Thankfully, she had thought to put her phone and driver's license in her pocket before she had gone up to her apartment. She fished the old-fashioned dumb phone out and took a deep breath. No choice. Nowhere to run. Nowhere to go. She scrolled through the contact list, stopping at one she had marked *** as her finger hovered over the call button. Decision made, she mashed out a quick message.

The Cabernet was fine, but the weather is getting too hot for red wine. I need something else.

She pressed send. Her contact would understand the code they had devised long ago. This was her last hope.

CHAPTER 1

"THANK YOU, THANK YOU, EVERYONE," Riva Lennox said as thundering applause greeted the end of her speech. "And though we've already formalized everything with the board yesterday, let me take this moment to pass the baton to my son, the new CEO of Lennox Corporation, Matthew Everett Lennox." More applause. "Son, go ahead and stand up—no, Jason, not you." The crowd laughed. "Yes, my identical twin sons can usually fool everyone, even me, sometimes; but I know when they're trying to pull a fast one on me. Jason always has that certain smile when he's up to something." More laughs. "Hopefully, you guys won't be pulling the old switcheroo since Jason will also be very busy running Lennox Foundation on his own."

Matthew Lennox looked up at his twin brother with a wry smile. His mother knew them so well.

"C'mon, dude," Jason urged, grabbing him by the elbow. "It's Mom and Dad's retirement party."

"Fine," he grumbled. Matthew stood up, pasted a smile on his face, and faced the audience, waving his hand.

"That's my boy," Riva said. "Now, to everyone here—and I'm sure I speak for my husband as well—from the bottom of my heart, thank you. It has been a pleasure being your President and CEO for almost three decades. Many of you credit me with turning Lennox Corp into what it is today, but I have to humbly disagree, as I could not have done it without all of you."

Matthew locked eyes with his father. Hank Lennox gave him a wink and then turned back to the stage, his eyes transfixed on his mate. Riva was perhaps too modest, as she did deserve most of the credit for turning what had been a dying family-run company into a large, multinational corporation. His mother was a brilliant businesswoman and not only ensured Lennox Corporation survived but also thrived. Though their primary product was still blackstone, the hardest substance on earth, his mother had broadened their portfolio into construction, transportation, and real estate. Despite her accomplishments, she still somehow managed to get home in time for dinner almost every night, plus never missed a recital, school play, or sports game in her children's lives. A lesser man might have been intimidated to take over for such a person, but, perhaps as his father had told him many times, Matthew was just as driven and business-minded as his mother, and having inherited his father's dragon side, was fierce and determined as his shifter animal. His mother said that it was a good combination.

Matthew had Lennox Corp in his blood, and working there was something he'd always dreamed of. Indeed, some of his happiest memories were of playing under her desk at the Lennox Corp headquarters or visiting the blackstone mines with his father. He graduated top of his class in college and went to a direct-track MBA program in one of the most prestigious schools in the country, all the while working part-time at a stock-trading company. He'd been officially working at Lennox for four years, but he'd lived and breathed the company his whole life. When Riva announced she was retiring at the end of the year, it was no surprise she appointed Matthew as her successor.

Riva finished her speech and then stepped down from the stage. Hank stood up and gathered her in his arms for a long, sensuous kiss.

"Eww, Mom, Dad, get a room!" Sybil, their youngest and only sister, joked. Beside her, their adopted brother, Luke, merely shrugged.

"Did you slip her the tongue?" Jason asked. "Way to go Dad! Someone's gonna get lucky ..."

"You do realize that's your mother you're talking about," Hank said when he pulled away. Riva's face with flush, and she looked around her sheepishly.

Still, no one was surprised. His parents were not just husband and wife but also mates. Though most shifters believed dragons rarely found mates, his father had somehow lucked out. She was human, of course, as the only way dragons could have dragonlings was with another of their kind or with a non-shifter. They'd been together for almost thirty years, and it seemed their bond and their love for each other only grew stronger each year.

"So, Mom, Dad, you guys ready for your 'round-the-world trip?" Jason asked.

"I think, after all these years, we deserve it," Hank said.

"And we're leaving everything in capable hands," Riva said, her eyes twinkling.

"Finally, the old generation can have some fun while you young ones do all the hard work," Hank added. He himself had retired from running the Lennox Foundation just six months before, handing over the reins to Jason. While some may say Matthew was the more serious and driven twin, Jason was not without his talents. His good nature and the fact that he was approachable and friendly made him a good match for the job. People naturally gravitated to his more affable twin.

"We'll miss you, Daddy," Sybil said, wrapping her arms around Hank. "But you guys will have fun, I'm sure."

"Aunt Riva, Uncle Hank, congratulations." Ben Walker, their cousin, held his arms out as he walked toward their table. He engulfed Riva in a big hug and then shook hands with Hank. "I'm sure Mom and Dad will be thrilled you'll be joining them."

Ben's parents had retired six months ago and were now on their own trip, traveling around the country in an RV with another couple, Clark and Martha Caldwell. The three couples were the best of friends, and it only made sense they wanted to spend their twilight years together, seeing as all their children were grown.

"They're in Los Angeles, just waiting for us," Hank said. "First stop on our trip is Tokyo."

As more people came to their table to congratulate them, Matthew quietly slipped away from the ballroom of the Blackstone Grand Hotel where the party was taking place. He headed to the double doors leading out to the balcony. Once outside, he enjoyed the fresh mountain air. From out here in the valley, he could see the Blackstone Mountains. His home.

"Yo, bro, what are you doing out here alone?" Jason said as he walked up behind him. "Are you doing that broody shit again? I know the ladies dig it, but this is taking it too far. Come in and celebrate!"

"It's not my party," he said with a shrug.

Jason stood next to him on the balcony, then turned to him. Matthew was used to this, looking at another person and seeing his own face reflected back. They were the same, yet so different, his mother would often say.

"Maybe we'll have to plan a welcome party for you." Jason must have seen the distaste on his face because he laughed. "Or not. You know, the only person who hates other people more than you is Luke."

Matthew had to admit there was some truth to that. Their adopted brother was a solitary creature, in more ways than one. "I don't hate people," Matthew said. "I just don't like them as much as you do."

"Now that, I won't deny." Jason chuckled. "C'mon, I think Mom and Dad are ready to head to the airport."

"I'll be in in a minute."

As the balcony doors closed, Matthew thought about his brother's words. He didn't exactly *hate* people. His father said he was an old soul, even when he was young. While Jason preferred to play outdoors (and, later, go out to bars and cause trouble with his best friend Nate), Matthew wanted nothing more than to stay home and read or study. He felt most comfortable surrounded by his books and computers, looking at stock prices or balance sheets. Not that he didn't go out. He was up for a beer with his friends every now and then, and he was never short of female company. But, lately, especially since his mother had announced she was going to retire, he felt the enormous pressure of preserving their family legacy.

It wasn't that his parents put that pressure on him. No, Riva and Hank would have been just as happy to hand over the reigns to someone else and support him in whatever he pursued. He put the pressure on himself, to not fuck up. He wanted to make Lennox Corp even bigger and better than before.

Matthew took one last look at the mountains and headed inside. There was already a small crowd of well-wishers by the lobby front door, and he jogged over to make sure he didn't miss saying goodbye to his folks.

"There you are," Riva said when her eyes landed on him. She pulled him close for a hug. "Take care of everything, my sweet boy."

"I'll take care of the company, Mom," he promised.

"No, I mean take care of yourself," she reprimanded. "And try to get out more, please? No woman is going to want a workaholic for a husband."

"Mom ..."

"Aww, c'mon, is it too early to be asking for grandchildren?" she said.

"Maybe Jason's got a few floating around we don't know about," Sybil quipped.

"Hey," his brother protested. "I'm pretty sure we'd know if I did!"

"I just want the best for you," Riva said, her eyes darting to Luke. "All of you."

"Riva, we'll be late," Hank reminded her.

She took a deep breath. "Well, we're off! We'll call every day."

"Mom, just update your Facebook so we know you're alive," Sybil said, rolling her eyes. "Or text. No one calls these days. Unless you want to Facetime."

"Fine," Riva said and put her arms around her daughter. "Stay safe, all of you."

"You do know all your children are shifters, right?" Jason

joked and wrapped his mother in a hug and lifted her off her feet. "Bye Mom, Dad, have a great trip."

"You deserve all of this, mom," Matthew said when it was his turn to hug her.

When Matthew let go, she turned to Luke. "You take care of yourself, Luke," she said, looking up at him. She put her arms around him in an awkward hug.

"I will, Riva." He nodded.

Matthew noticed his mother's expression falter for a second, then turn back into a bright smile, but she said nothing. It didn't escape Jason's attention either, and his brother clenched his fist and gritted his teeth. He put a hand on his twin's shoulder and sent him a warning look. What happened was in the past, and Riva never had any hard feelings. Luke would always be her son, she said to them. Nothing would change that.

Hank tugged on Riva's hand, and she gave them one last smile as they climbed into the limo. All the well-wishers waved at them as they drove away.

"Well, this was fun, but I have to get home," Sybil said. "Early meeting tomorrow. See you guys!"

"Drive carefully," Matthew warned. "And let us know when you're safe at home."

"I will, *Mom*," she said, rolling her eyes. "Bye!" She waved at them and then headed to the elevators.

"So, now that the parents are gone, what do you say we head out to The Den," Jason said.

"We're not fifteen, you know," Matthew pointed out. "You can go to the bar anytime."

Jason put his arm around his shoulders. "I said 'we.' You're coming with us."

Matthew shook his head. "No, I have too much—"

"Are we headed to the Den?" Nate Caldwell said as he popped up behind Matthew. The wolf shifter had a big grin on his face. "All right!"

"No, *you* guys are going to The Den," Matthew said. "I'm going home."

"Aww, c'mon," Jason said. "Ben is coming." He waved to their cousin, who was talking to some Lennox Corp employees across the room. He smiled back and gave them a thumbs up.

"And Luke too," Nate added.

"Luke?" Matthew frowned. Looking around, he didn't see a sign of his other brother. "You got Luke to come out with you?"

"Yeah, he's bringing the car around. He's gonna be our designated driver," Nate said.

"How much do you plan to drink?" It took a hell of a lot of liquor to get a shifter drunk.

"I think he's just looking out for us," Nate replied.

"C'mon, Matthew. You've been working 80-hour weeks for months!" Jason exclaimed. "You deserve a break. You can work more when you start as CEO on Monday. But it's a Friday night, and you deserve some fun."

Matthew thought for a moment. "Fine. One drink." Then he'd head back to Blackstone Castle. "And I'll drive myself."

"Great!" Jason and Nathan high-fived.

"There's a hot new bartender," Nathan said. "Saw her last night. She's smokin'. And new in town."

"So, you haven't banged her yet?" Jason asked.

"And neither have you," Nate retorted.

Matthew rolled his eyes. To say that Jason and Nate had a reputation around town was an understatement. Not that he could blame them. They were both single, young, good-looking and could charm the pants off any woman under ninety. And both his brother and his friend enjoyed every single minute of their bachelorhood. Personally, though, that wasn't Matthew's style.

"C'mon, let's go." The sooner they got to The Den, the sooner he'd be able to leave.

CHAPTER 2

"HUSTLE UP," Tim Grimes, the owner of The Den, said in his usual gruff voice. "It's Friday night, and we're gonna be real busy soon."

Catherine gave Tim a two-fingered salute. "Aye, aye, Captain!" She tried to move the keg under the bar, but she only managed to push it a few inches.

Tim let out a grunt and gently moved her aside. With one hand, he lifted it up effortlessly and placed it under the taps. "Now, get that hooked up."

"Will do," she said cheerfully, which only earned her another grunt. She chuckled to herself. Tim may look like a grumpy old mountain man with his thick white beard, suspenders, and propensity to dress in flannel, but she knew he was as soft as a marshmallow inside. After all, he'd not only given her this job but also helped her find a place to stay, despite having only met her four days ago.

Catherine tapped the keg with practiced ease. Satisfied with her work, she got up and began to wipe down the bar.

She was already done with all the prep and busy work, and, just as Tim had said, people started pouring in.

As orders from both the bar and tables came in, she got into the zone. Her Zen space, as she called. After a year of tending bar, she'd gotten used to the rhythm of making and serving drinks. In fact, most nights seemed to melt into each other. Same shit, different night.

Still, it was good money for someone with no other marketable skills, and who knew she would be so good at it? She smiled, chatted and flirted with the customers, though that was one part of the job that came naturally to her. She chuckled to herself, thinking of that first night she had somehow conned her way into her first bartending job. She had mixed up the drink orders, gotten herself into the weeds, and nearly got fired. If it wasn't for Rissa helping her out—

No.

She shut down that part of her brain as her throat began to constrict with unshed tears for her friend. *Get back into the Zen space.* Taking a deep breath, she turned around and went back to work, pushing all other thoughts aside.

She continued to sling the drinks, the work keeping her mind steady. Before she knew it, she was already halfway through her shift.

"Not bad, new girl," Heather, one of the waitresses, said as she put her tray on the counter. "Didn't think you could handle yourself, but you're doing all right."

"Thanks," she said. "Keep 'em coming."

"Oh, my. Best step up your game."

"Hmmm?" What did she mean?

Heather nodded to the front door. "They're here. Oh, and looks like they're out in full force."

"Who?"

Heather giggled. "You'll find out soon enough."

Catherine's head whipped toward the front door, craning her neck to see what Heather was talking about. There were a couple of guys standing there, eyes scanning the room, probably for an empty spot. A group of guys going to a bar wasn't unusual, but there was something about them that seemed different. Sure, it looked like they had come from some fancy party in their tuxes, but that wasn't it. All of them were tall, gorgeous, and looked like they had stepped out of a men's magazine. They also had this aura that seemed to fill the room and make people stare at them. An animal magnetism that made every pair of eyes turn toward them (especially the female ones).

The first guy had longish, light brown hair; a handsome face; and an easy smile. He was tall and lean, though the guy behind was much taller. And bigger. The blond man with the thick beard was broad around the shoulders and undoubtedly the tallest man she'd ever seen. Maybe six-foot-seven at least. Next was the dark-haired man, probably the same height as the first man. Everyone seemed to know him. He shook hands with a couple of people as they made their way to an empty table in the corner.

The fourth man in the group seemed to have the opposite effect. People gave him a wide berth and avoided his gaze. She supposed he was just as handsome as his companions, with his long blond hair and thick beard, but the scowl on his face definitely gave that "leave-me-the-fuck-alone" vibe.

Catherine was about to return to a drink she was making when she felt the hairs on the back of her neck stand on end. Looking toward the group, she realized a fifth man had joined them.

Even from afar, she could tell he was different. It wasn't

just the way he carried himself; it was *something* about him. While his friends were all good-looking, he was drop-dead *gorgeous*. He had midnight black hair that looked like it had been perfectly combed, but was now deliciously ruffled; tanned skin, like he was used to being outdoors; and, under his white tuxedo shirt, his muscles stretched and flexed. And those eyes. They were a grey so light they were almost silver. And they were also staring right back at her.

She gasped and grabbed the side of the bar as she stumbled and looked away. Did she forget to breathe? Heat crept up her neck. She glanced back at him. He was still staring at her.

The way he looked at her sent her senses tingling. *Shifter.* But *what* was he?

"Catherine!" Tim called. "I've been calling you for the last five seconds. What the hell's the matter with you?"

Tearing her gaze away from the man, she quickly snapped out of her trance. Unfortunately, that also sent the glass in her hand tumbling to the floor. "Sorry, Boss!" she stammered. "I'll take care of that." She grabbed the broom and mop from the corner and quickly cleaned up the mess. It didn't take her too long, but by the time she finished, the line at the bar was already two deep, and she still had to finish the table orders.

Oh, fuck me.

What was the matter with her? Sure, that guy was gorgeous, but she'd never had that kind of reaction to a man. Maybe she had eaten something weird. That ham sandwich for lunch maybe?

"Sorry for the wait," she said to the next person in line. She didn't bother looking at him as she grabbed a clean rag from under the bar.

"No worries, sweetheart," the man said, his green eyes twinkling.

She realized he was the first guy from that group, the sandy-haired one. Beside him was his friend, the dark-haired guy everyone seemed to know. *Hmmm.* He looked familiar somehow. Again, her senses went tingling. They were shifters, too.

Most humans didn't know how to tell if someone was a shifter, at least they didn't bother to learn. But Catherine knew what to look for. It was that look in their eyes. It wasn't something she could explain, but she just knew.

"So, what can I get you?" she said, pasting a sunny smile on her face.

"Five shots of tequila, five shots of whiskey, five shots of bourbon, and your phone number," the first man said.

Oh boy, like I hadn't heard that one before. "Gotcha," she said and began to prepare the drinks. As she placed everything on a tray, the other man put his black credit card on the bar. *Ooh, Mr. Bigshot.*

The man frowned. "Hey, you're missing something."

"Huh?"

"Your phone number," he said cheekily.

Catherine placed her hands on her hips. "Well, I can't very well give all of you my phone number, can I? Wouldn't want you to fight over me. What's that saying? Bros before hos?"

He put his hand on his chest and dropped his jaw. "I'm shocked. In this day and age you would refer to yourself in those terms? I thought with feminism and everything ..." He shook his head.

She giggled. She had to admit he was pretty damn funny. "Sorry, I don't date customers. Hey!" She made a grab for the credit card as he swiped it off the table.

"Oh, so you'll give this to me for free, huh?"

As funny as she thought he was, she had a job to do. She

held out her hand and gave him her best don't-mess-with-me look. He flashed her a smile and gave her back the card.

"I'm Jason. Lennox."

"Uh-huh," she said as she ran the card. "I know how to read."

"And I'm Nathan," the other guy said. "I'm not as rich as my friend here, but I'm talented in other ways." He raised an eyebrow at her.

She handed the card and slip to Jason. "Really? Can you stick it up your own ass?"

That made Nathan throw his head back and laugh, a move that surprised her. Most guys would get all huffy or angry, but it seemed these guys could take it as much as they could dish out.

"Oh burn!" Jason laughed. "I like you."

"And I feel somewhat lukewarm toward you but only because of that tip you signed on your card." She raised her hand to stop him. "Please, gentlemen, no more dick jokes. In this job, I've heard them all, trust me."

"You're an okay gal," Nathan said. "What's your name again?"

The people behind them were starting to roll their eyes, and, as much as she enjoyed the banter, she had a job to do. "Catherine."

"I guess we'll see you around." The two of them flashed her mischievous smiles and took their tray of drinks back to their table.

Catherine continued to sling drinks but kept the table in the corner of her eye. She could have sworn that gorgeous guy was looking at her, but she didn't have a second to stop and make sure. The entire time, though, she felt that prickling on the back of her neck like someone was watching her.

"So, you've met Jason Lennox and Nathan Caldwell," Heather said when she came back. "Those boys are trouble, I'm warning you."

"I handled them pretty well."

"And I'm proud of you. Still, it's rare to see all five boys together, and it's usually just those two causin' trouble here," Heather said. "Those shifter boys. But," Heather continued, "some of the girls around here—especially the ones who drive up from the big cities—you know they're the ones looking for trouble. And those boys attract them like flies to honey."

"Oh? Are they all … brothers or something?" Before she could ask *"who's the hunky one,"* she bit her lip.

"Not all of them. Nathan's the only one not related to them. Jason, you've met. Matthew's obviously his brother, and so's Luke. Ben—he's the big guy—he's their cousin or something."

"Wait, back up. Who're the brothers?" She was confused. None of those men looked that much alike to her.

"Duh, Jason and Matthew, but Luke's their adopted brother." She pointed to the scowling guy with long hair who was ambling toward the bathroom.

"Oh, they're brothers?" she said, nodding at the two dark-haired men who were deep in conversation, their heads close together.

Heather looked at her strangely. "Girl, you need to get your eyes checked or something?"

"Hmmm … I guess the eyes are the same." Silvery gray, like pools of molten steel.

"Duh, they're identical twins—oh shoot, Boss is giving me the stink eye. Sorry, gotta go." Heather quickly walked away.

"Twins?" Catherine said aloud to no one in particular. No way those two were twins. Maybe the same body type and hair, but... "Must be some small town joke," she huffed. Then she realized Heather has said the hunky guy's name. *Matthew.* She wanted to say it out loud, wondering if it would cause the same chills she got just thinking about it. And him. And wondering what his hands would feel like—

"Get a grip," she told herself. This wasn't the time nor place. She had come here to maintain a low profile, keep her head down, and not get involved with anyone. Just passing the time until it was safe to move on.

CHAPTER 3

"MATTHEW, ARE YOU OKAY?" Meg asked, as she put the tray of coffee and cakes on his desk.

"Huh?" Matthew looked up at their housekeeper standing over him as he sat there, staring out the window. She wiped her hand on her khakis, then placed it on her hip.

"Matthew Everett Lennox, what is wrong with you today?" Meg said, concern on her face. Most employers might have bristled at her tone, but Meg wasn't just their housekeeper. She was family, and Matthew and Jason treated her like their second mother. Though she was married to their butler, Christopher, the two never had kids of their own and thus spoiled all the Lennox children.

"I'm fine," he grumbled, then grabbed the lemon poppy seed cake from the plate and bit into it. "Thank you, Meg."

"I was calling you for lunch, and you ignored me. Now, I walk in here unannounced, and you barely notice I'm here." She raised a brow at him. "Care to tell me what's on your mind?"

He swallowed the bite of cake in one gulp. *I don't think so,* he wanted to say. Meg probably wouldn't want to know what was occupying his mind at that moment, so he lied. "I have an important meeting on Monday. My first as CEO of Lennox Corp."

"Well, Monday's still two days away and today's Saturday. I can't believe you'd rather spend your time locked up in your office on your day off. You're worse than your mother, you know," she lectured.

"I'll be fine. I'll finish this snack and then leave the office, okay?" He stood up, put an arm around Meg, and walked her to the door. "I'm fine. I promise."

Meg nodded. "I'll be watching this door, Matthew," she warned before leaving.

When the door closed, Matthew took a deep breath and softly banged his forehead on the wood. What was wrong with him? He wished he knew. He was pretty sure he was perfectly fine and normal until he walked into The Den last night.

Until he saw *her*.

Even from the across the room, something about her made it difficult to look away. Sure, she was gorgeous, blond, and had curves that could make a man weep, but he'd had his share of beautiful women over the years. But this one ... he hadn't even approached her yet, and he was drawn to her. From afar, he could see the depth of her blue eyes, drawing him in like a siren's song. He stood there, staring at her like some idiot.

And she was staring right back. Who was she?

Nathan and Jason confirmed she was the hot new bartender they'd been talking about. Matthew loved both of them more than his own life, but at that moment, he wanted to deck them and break their noses. His dragon, normally silent and calm, roared in fury, and, for a moment, all four men looked at him.

"Matthew, are you alright?" Ben had asked, concern in his eyes.

"I'm fine."

"Oh yeah? Then why do you look like you're ready to break this table in half?" Luke said.

His adopted brother was more observant than the others, that was for sure. Maybe his lion had sensed his anger.

God, he didn't even know her name and couldn't bring himself to ask Jason or Nathan. If they noticed him staring at her, they didn't say anything. Luke had given him a strange look, but he noticed everything. He wondered if his brother also noticed how his claws scratched the leather seats whenever some guy stared at the buxom bartender too long or when his eyes strayed down below her neck.

He had to get this out of his system … whatever it was. Maybe if he went to see her, it would go away. He'd see some flaw in her, something that would make him forget about her.

CHAPTER 4

SATURDAY NIGHT at The Den wasn't as busy as Friday, but it was still packed. Heather told Catherine they mostly get out-of-towners during the weekends, especially once the busy tourist season began. Blackstone didn't offer the biggest or best slopes in the area, but the picturesque Main Street attracted lots of families who wanted to take pictures, go shopping, or just walk around. Of course, it didn't hurt that there was a big shifter population in town, and though they weren't tourist attractions themselves, it drew a lot of curious folks.

"And some other type of folk," Heather added, rolling her eyes at a group of girls dressed in skimpy outfits, their hair curled and teased within an inch of their lives.

"What do you mean?" Catherine asked.

Heather lowered her voice. "Shifter groupies. You know, girls who want to know what it's like to be with a shifter."

"Oh." Catherine frowned.

"Don't be a prude, hon," Heather said. "I've tried it, too! It's definitely an experience."

"I'm not a prude," she said. "I just ... don't know how I feel about it. On the one hand—yay feminism, right? Women should be free to explore their sexuality without being labeled as sluts. But on the other hand, shifters aren't some carnival ride you try once and then get off."

"Honey," she nodded at the group of men eyeing the women, "those guys definitely don't feel like they're being exploited."

Catherine flashed her a wry smile. "You know what I mean."

"How 'bout you, honey," Heather asked with a wink. "You wanna climb on that and get off?"

She gave Heather a nervous laugh. "Ha! Right." She swallowed hard and turned around, busying herself at the sink, hoping her friend wouldn't see how red her cheeks were.

When she got home last night after her shift, she couldn't sleep. Whenever she closed her eyes, all she could see were those light silver eyes staring at her. Finally, curiosity had gotten the best of her, and she googled him. Matthew Lennox.

Catherine hadn't quite decided if it was a good move or not. What she saw shook her to her core. Matthew Lennox wasn't just rich. His family practically owned the town, and he was the new CEO of one of the largest companies in the country. But that wasn't what concerned Catherine. No, it was the fact that he was a shifter. A dragon shifter, one of the few left in the world.

A shiver ran down her back just thinking about it. She should have done more research on Blackstone before deciding to come here. That night she decided to leave L.A. was a blur to her. She wasn't thinking straight. The only thing she knew was that she wanted to go away to somewhere safe. Doing the opposite of what people expected had kept her under the radar for a year while she lived in LA, so she thought it would work the second time she decided to run.

Blackstone was a town full of shifters. It was the last place other shifters would look for her. If she could just keep her head down and stay unnoticed, maybe the Chesnovak Brotherhood Pride would never find her here or even think of looking for her in Blackstone. Besides, shifters were territorial, right? They probably wouldn't take too kindly to lion mafia shifters coming to their town.

But a dragon shifter bazillionaire CEO? Talk about attracting attention. She let out a long sigh. Well, it wasn't like she was going to see him anytime soon. He didn't even come up to the bar to get a drink last night. Not that she was disappointed or anything. Not at all.

Pushing those thoughts aside, she continued making and serving drinks. Her tip jar was looking mighty full, a fact that made her sigh in relief. Having left everything behind, her closet and even most of the apartment were almost empty. Including the spot under her mattress where she kept her meager life savings. Her "contact" didn't have a safe way to send her a lot of cash, though he was able to provide her with transport away from Los Angeles. She had driven the car east as far as she could go with a full tank, sold it to the first car lot she had found, and then bought a bus ticket to Colorado. She was on her last couple hundred dollars when she came into town, just enough to pay for a few groceries and her week's rent on the place Tim had helped her find. If the busy tourist season was coming up, it could mean more cash. She just had to ride it out until she figured out her next move.

"Well, that's a sight for sore eyes," one of the other waitresses, Olive, said, giving an exaggerated whistle and a nod across the room.

"What?" She followed Olive's gaze, and her stomach did a flip-flop when her eyes landed on Matthew Lennox, standing by himself at one of the cocktail tables, his gaze fixed on her. She wasn't sure if it was because he was closer this time or because he was a dragon shifter, but she swore she could literally feel the heat of his gaze.

"Hmmm, he keeps staring over here," Olive said and flipped her long red locks over her shoulder. "I should go see what he wants." She put her hands on her breasts and pushed them up to make her cleavage bigger, then sauntered over to Matthew.

An irritation pricked at Catherine, but she wasn't sure why or where it was coming from. Nonetheless, she had this urge to rip Olive's hair extensions out of her head. The feeling grew and made her chest tighten as she watched Olive lean over when she was taking Matthew's order.

"Excuse me. *Excuse me.*"

Catherine snapped out of her trance. "Oh, sorry," she said to the young woman waiting at the bar, her face drawn into an irate expression. She quickly took the woman's order, made her drink, and moved on to the next customer, all the while very aware of (and ignoring) the gaze boring into her.

It took all of Matthew's strength to keep his claws from slashing even more of the furniture inside The Den. *Shit, I should really send a check to Tim.* But he couldn't help it.

Last night was bad enough, but tonight was worse. Before, most of the guys flirting with her were from Blackstone, and they knew Tim. They would never try anything to disrespect him or his employees. But tonight, these out-of-towner pieces of shit were much bolder. They didn't know Tim or care about what other people in town thought of them.

A group of guys, probably frat boys from one of the college towns nearby, walked in about an hour ago and stayed at the bar. Or more like staked their territory. They never left and made it impossible for anyone else to get near it. And they manipulated the bartender's attention, joking and laughing with her, their eyes raking over her cleavage and God knows what else whenever she turned around and bent over to get something from under the bar.

His blood boiled, and shot after shot of whiskey did nothing to calm him. A couple of those shifter groupies had been giving him the eye, and for a moment, he considered taking them up on their silent offer. It had been a while since he'd been with a woman because he had been too busy the past couple of weeks. But none of the groupies appealed to him. In fact, his dragon was clawing at him each time he considered it. It wanted only one woman.

Matthew considered physically pulling those men away, but it probably wasn't a good idea. He was a CEO now, and he could just imagine the gossip that would spread through town the next day.

"Fuck this," he said out loud. He dropped a couple of bills on the table and walked to the exit.

He got all the way to the parking lot and into his Range Rover, but couldn't bring himself to start the car. His fucking dragon wouldn't let him leave; it was clawing and roaring at him. "Goddammit," he cursed, slamming his palms on the wheel. He and his dragon spent his entire life getting along and now this? Was he getting some weird shifter disease? That same tumor that had killed his grandfather?

Matthew sat in the car, stewing in his juices. He waited,

watching as patrons began to stumble out of The Den. Watching as it started to empty and the lights inside began to turn off one at a time to signal the remaining customers that it was closing time. Finally, the last of them walked out. It was those frat boys.

"Thank fuck," he muttered to himself. As he slipped the key into the ignition, he stopped. He saw five of them walk out of the bar. But hadn't there been six? A dreaded feeling crept into his chest.

His body tensed, waiting. Counting the seconds. The last of the lights turned off outside along with the neon sign. Then, the door opened. It was her. She walked out, bundled up in a puffy coat with her purse slung over her shoulder. There were a few remaining cars in the lot, but she didn't walk to any of them.

Where the hell is she going? Is she going to walk in this weather? Damn woman.

As he started the car, another vehicle pulled up beside her, blocking her way, as she was about to cross the street. He saw the window go down, and while he didn't see the driver's face, he could guess who it was. He must have said something to her, but she shook her head and then began walking away. *Good girl.*

But the driver wasn't taking no for an answer. He got out of the car, reached her in two steps, and grabbed her by the arm. She stumbled back, and he pushed her against the hood of the vehicle, trapping her with his arms.

"Bastard!" Matthew was out of the car in less than three seconds. His shifter side allowed him to move faster, even in his human form, and soon he was pulling the asshole off her. "Get. The Fuck. Away from her," he roared as he slammed the other man onto the ground, making him scream in pain.

A horrified gasp made him turn around. There she was, pretty face all ashen with wide blue eyes looking up at him.

Mine.

Matthew blinked. *What? Mine?*

Before he could react, a fist slamming into his side knocked the wind out of him, making him stagger back. *Fucking prick.* He quickly recovered and then grabbed the other man by the neck and lifted him off the ground.

"What the fuck is wrong with you?" he gasped. "You're ... choking ... me ..."

"Stop it! Put him down."

"Put him down?" he roared. Matthew let go of the man, letting him fall down.

"You freak!" he shouted as he scrambled up to his feet. "This town is full of you freaks."

"Yeah, well we don't want your kind here either," Matthew retorted. "Now get out."

The man yanked his car door open and slipped inside. "You'll pay for this, freak. Just you wait. You don't know who you're messing with."

"And you don't know who you're messing with. The name's Matthew Lennox. Look it up." He grabbed the driver's side door and slammed it so hard, the entire car shook. From outside, he saw the driver's face turn pale before the car peeled away.

"What ... what did you do?"

Matthew turned around to face her. For a second, he thought he was hallucinating. She was even more beautiful up close. Her golden hair surrounded her face like a halo, making her milky skin glow. Her eyes weren't just blue; they were the color of the sky on a bright day. This close, he could smell her sweet scent, and it was calling to him.

Mine.

There it was again. It wasn't just the inner voice, but a feeling. She was his. It was a feeling he knew deep in his bones. And he didn't even know her name.

The annoyed look remained on her face. Wait, was she … mad at him? For rescuing her from that creep?

"What did *I* do?" he asked in an incredulous voice. "How about thanking me for saving you?"

"Saving me?"

"Yeah. That bastard slammed you against his car. Had his hands all over you." The anger was bubbling up again, ready to burst at the mere memory of *anyone* touching her.

"I know self-defense," she said. "I was about to scream, and I'm sure Tim would have heard. He's a grizzly shifter, you know."

"Polar bear, actually," he corrected. Why was he arguing with her? "And you're welcome."

She harrumphed. "Fine. *Thanks.*" She turned around and began walking away.

"Hey!" Where the hell was she going? Using his shifter speed, he got in front of her, blocking her path.

"What are you doing?"

"I'm taking you home."

Sky blue eyes went wide as dinner plates. "Excuse me?"

"To your home," he corrected. They could talk about her moving in with him another time. Maybe he should iron out other important details first. Like her name. "I'm Matthew Lennox."

"I know who you are," she said, crossing her arms over her chest.

"Usually, when someone introduces himself, you should do the same."

She paused and huffed. "Catherine. Archer."

There was something off with her voice, a slight accent that would have been indiscernible to anyone else, and one he couldn't place. British? "Where are you from?"

"Listen, I'm freezing my ass off here; I don't have time for this." She turned around, but he blocked her way again. She let out a frustrated yelp. "Stop doing that!"

"I said I'm taking you home. My car's over there."

"You've done nothing but stare at me like some creepy stalker all night. Why the hell would I jump into your car?"

He supposed she was right. "Okay, fine. Just … let me walk you home then. Or follow you home and make sure you're safe. I promise I'll stay at least five steps away."

Her shoulders sank in defeat, and she gritted her teeth. "Fine. But don't stay behind me like some creeper. I don't turn my back to …"

"Animals?" he finished.

"Strangers," she said. She turned around, and he stepped beside her, following her as she crossed the street. He wanted to switch to the other side when they got halfway, but she looked skittish enough that he was afraid to make any sudden moves. Despite her confidence, he could smell the apprehension rolling off her.

When they crossed to the other side, she stopped in front of the first building. "Okay, we're here."

"What?" He looked up at the small, two-story building that housed the local hardware store. "You live here?"

"Up there," she said, nodding to the second floor. "Tim helped me get this place. It's kinda shitty, but I can't beat the commute." She fished her keys out of her pocket. "You can go now."

"Go out with me."

"Excuse me?"

The words had come out faster than he expected. In hindsight, he probably should have been smoother. "Dinner. Tomorrow night. You eat, right?"

"Yes, I eat but ..."

"Then come out and eat with me."

"I just met you five seconds ago," she said. "I'm not going out with you."

"But how am I supposed to get to know you better if you don't go out with me?"

"That's not the point."

"I think that *is* the point."

She let out a frustrated groan and slipped her key into the lock. "Look, I'm not looking for anyone right now."

"I just want to sit down and have a meal with you. I'm not asking you to marry me." *Yet.*

The lock clicked, and she opened the door an inch. Matthew resisted the urge to push her inside and kiss her against the wall, even though her sweet scent was driving him crazy.

"I can't," she said without turning around. "Th-thank you for getting rid of that guy." With that, she stepped in and closed the door. The lock clicking into place echoed in his ears.

Matthew stood there, just staring at the door. If he wanted to, no door could keep him out. But he had to respect her wishes. If only there was some sort of textbook or report he could read to analyze the situation and figure out what to do.

He'd just have to wing it.

CHAPTER 5

THE MOMENT MATTHEW stepped into The Den a few days later, he had second thoughts about this winging-it plan.

Catherine's initial rejection had stung, but he was determined to win her over. Fighting the urge to see her as soon as possible, he gave her space. It had been two days since the night he had asked her out. He threw himself into work, as he wanted to make sure his first couple of days as CEO went smoothly.

Of course, he couldn't stop thinking about Catherine. Her face popped into his mind whenever he had a free moment, and so he filled every second he could. He was a beast at work, driving most of his staff to the edge. He was irritable and moody, and by the end of his first day, few of them approached him. By the end of the second day, his new assistant (hired just the day before) quit. No, things were not going well, and if he didn't get a hold of himself, he might turn into a literal beast at the office. That probably wouldn't be great for their stock price.

For the sake of his and his employees' sanity, he had to

find a way to control his dragon, which meant giving it what it wanted. Or rather, who it wanted.

Mine. Mine.

He had to laugh at the irony. Women had been throwing themselves at him most of his life. And now, the one woman he was desperate to have wanted nothing to do with him. More determined than ever, he thought he'd put the wing-it plan in motion.

But he didn't expect his brother and his friends to be at The Den. He couldn't even walk away and pretend he didn't see them.

This complicated things. Well, not really, but he couldn't count on them to *not* be assholes about the whole Catherine thing. Jason would probably rib him the hardest.

"Well, look who's here," Jason said as Matthew walked up to their usual table. "The prodigal son returns."

"I don't think that's how the story went," he said wryly.

"I thought now that you're CEO and everything, you'd forgotten about us," Nathan said in a mocked miffed tone. As usual, Luke remained silent but gave him an acknowledging nod as he sipped his beer.

"Aww, c'mon, maybe he needs some stress relief or somethin'," Ben said. "Want a beer, bud?"

Matthew nodded. "Sure."

Ben signaled the waitress and ordered a round of beers. Matthew followed her as she walked back to the bar. Maybe he'd misdirect them and make them think he was looking at her. But, really, his gaze was fixed on the bartender.

There she was. Catherine, as usual, was standing behind the bar. She took their waitress' orders with a quick nod and hurried back to the people waiting for their drinks.

"Aww, Nate, no," Jason said with a groan. "She's said no to you, like, a million times already."

"Just five times," Nathan said, rolling up his sleeves. "I'd say sixth time's a charm."

"Sixth time for who?" Matthew asked.

"The bartender," Jason said, nodding his head toward Catherine. "He's asked her out five times. She turned him down flat every single time. Jeez, even I know when to give up."

"That's because she hasn't heard the rumor about how my dick's bigger than all of yours. When she sees—" Nathan didn't finish his sentence because Matthew grabbed him by the shoulder and slammed him against the wall. "What the hell, man?!" Nathan quickly composed himself and hunched forward. His eyes glowed an eerie green, indicating the presence of his wolf, but Matthew didn't care. His dragon roared inside him in anger.

"Matt, what the fuck man?" Jason pulled him off, then stood between him and Nathan, probably knowing Matthew would never hurt his own brother. "You need to calm down; you're putting everyone on edge."

He looked around, and most of the shifters were looking at him warily, probably fully aware of the presence of his dragon. Even Tim, who was across the room, narrowed his eyes at him.

"I'm fine," he said, then turned to Nathan. "You stay away from her from now on," he warned.

Nathan's face scrunched up. "Yeah, man, whatever. Bros before—" But he didn't finish his sentence as Matthew let out another snarl, then turned away.

Matthew dragged his fingers through his hair. What the hell

was the matter with him? Nathan was like a brother to him, and the Lennoxes owed a lot to his family. But he had nearly ripped the wolf shifter's head off just for trying to ask Catherine out.

He walked over to the bar where two guys were hanging around, chatting and flirting with her. She seemed to enjoy the banter. Her laughter was like tinkling bells.

"Excuse me," he said through gritted teeth.

Two pairs of eyes swung over to him. He was getting ready for a fight, but their eyes widened in recognition.

"Hey, Jason!" one of them greeted. A young kid, maybe no more than twenty based on the soda in his hand. "Wow, I didn't think you'd hang out in places like this!" He stood up and shook his hand.

"Uh yes …"

"It's us! Colton and Jimmy." He gestured to his friend. "We work for you up in the mines. You welcomed us this morning; told us we were doing a good job."

"Oh right, yes." He nodded. Jason was scheduled to work in the mines today; that's probably why they thought he was his brother. He scented fur from the two men … hmmm … the big one, Colton, was probably a bear, and his friend smelled like a feline. Mountain lion or panther, he'd guess.

"Really glad to be part of the team," Jimmy said.

"Uh, yes … same here." He shook hands with both of them, unsure of what to do now. He was ready to fight them off, but they seemed to be good guys. His guys, apparently. "Yes, well, do you mind?" He gestured to the bar.

"Of course not! Can we get you a drink?" Colton called Catherine over. "Hey Cat, one beer for the boss over here."

Catherine's jaw dropped, but she just shrugged and said nothing as she reached for a beer in the cooler.

"Hey, no need ... uh, thanks," he said as Colton handed him a cold bottle.

"Of course! Anything we can do for you, just say it."

Hmmm. "Well, boys," he said, as he sat down at the bar. "There is one thing." He winked at Catherine. "Would you mind giving us some privacy?"

"What? Oh yeah, sure thing!" Colton said. As he turned away from Catherine, he gave Matthew a wink and mouthed *good luck*. He gave him a pat on the shoulder as both men walked away.

"Wow, must be good to be the boss," she said, rolling her eyes.

"Why yes, it is," he replied.

"You get free stuff even though you're already rich, and you can tell people to go away when you want to."

"Hey, they gave me the beer," he said, putting his hands up. "And as for the other thing ... well, I wanted to talk to you. Have dinner—"

"I thought your name was Matthew," she interrupted. "Why did they call you Jason?"

"Oh you know, we get mixed up all the time." He shrugged, not really wanting to talk about his brother.

She frowned. "People here are strange. I thought shifters were supposed to have good eyesight or something."

"Huh?" *What was she talking about?* "Listen, I want to ask you—"

"Sorry," she nodded to the people who sat at the bar, "I'm working." She walked over to the waiting customers.

Matthew peered at them. Unfortunately, he didn't know these guys and couldn't just ask them to leave. But maybe he could persuade them.

"Good evening, gentlemen," he said. "Can I buy you your drinks?"

"What?" one of them said.

"Sure!" another interjected. "What do you want in return?"

"Nothing. Just … take your drinks and go." He put his black card on the table and slid it over to Catherine. "Just put it on this one, sweetheart," he said, giving her a wink.

She frowned at him, but took the card and ran it. "Here you go," she said. When the group walked away with their free drinks, he gave her a smirk. "Are you planning on buying everyone's drinks?"

"I wasn't, but now that you mention it …" *Sounds like a plan.*

"Arghh!" She threw her hands up and busied herself in the far corner.

Matthew interrogated every person who came to the bar, took their drink order, and passed it along to Catherine, ensuring none of them talked to her. Most of the guys shrugged and went on their way, but the few who tried to protest usually went away with their tails between their legs when he gave them his most intimidating I-can-literally-eat-you-whole look.

"You have to stop this," Catherine said. "You can't keep doing this. I'm going to talk to Tim."

"He's still making money," Matthew pointed out. "And I made sure to tip you double each drink.'

Her pretty face went red. "Take it back."

"Only if you go out—"

"No!" She slammed her hands on the bar. Her eyes went stormy, and her chest heaved with each breath. The only thing he could think of was reaching over and grabbing her for a kiss.

"Hey now, what's going on here?"

Christ.

Jason.

"I heard you were buying drinks for everyone," Jason said with a lopsided smile. He slid onto the stool next to him and put an arm around him. "Mighty generous of you, bro."

"Will you tell him to please leave?" Catherine said, her eyes pleading.

"Is my brother bothering you? I'm shocked," he said, putting his hand on his chest like a scandalized debutante. "Normally, I'm the troublemaker. Which is why I love pretending to be him so I can get away with shit."

She let out a laugh. "Pretending to be him? How would that work?"

"Well, I know he doesn't have the best fashion sense, but I just wear the same clothes, like when we were young."

Her brows knitted. "Your mother dressed you alike when you were young?"

"Yeah, you know. Twins and all."

Her eyes darted from Jason to Matthew, her mouth open. "You're what?"

"Twins," Matthew repeated.

"People say I'm the better-looking one," Jason added with a smile.

"You guys are kidding, right?" She shook her head. "This town must really be mental."

"Wait a minute ..." Jason's eyes narrowed. "Are you saying ... we don't look alike?"

"Look, if you guys want to pretend to be twins, that's none of my business." Catherine untied the apron from her waist. "I'm taking my break. Tim!" she called to her boss, signaling that she was heading out.

Matthew watched her walk to the back room. *What the heck was she talking about? Pretend to be twins?*

"Oh. My. *Fucking*. God." Jason's eyes were wide as he looked at Matthew. "She's the one, isn't she?"

Mine.

"How the fuck …" Did Jason feel it, too? Shit, he didn't want to fight his brother for Catherine, but he would if that's what it took.

"Shit!" Jason slapped his thigh and let out a hoot. "She's yours. That's why you were going all caveman on her? Chasing off those guys?"

"How the hell did you know?" He sulked.

"Dude," he put an arm around his shoulder, "don't you ever listen to what Mom says? About girls?"

"You take girl advice from Mom?"

"Shit, no! Not the kind I'm interested in. I mean, you know, how she blathers on about her mother's family and twins."

Hmmm … he did remember her saying something about a legend with twins. He wracked his brain, trying to remember her words.

Jason let out an exaggerated groan. "I swear, and they say you're the smart one. She said, and I quote, 'the one who knows you from your twin is your soulmate.' I never understood it all this time, but I guess she meant it *literally*."

"Soulmate?" But humans didn't have magic, except for maybe witches and warlocks. "That can't be. No one else can tell us apart, not even mom."

"Yeah, no shit." He glanced at the back door. "What the hell have you been waiting for? Why aren't you making her yours? Doesn't your dragon think she's your mate?"

"*Fuck me.*" That's what his dragon was trying to tell him. Catherine was his. His *mate.* "Goddamn."

"What's the problem now?"

"She doesn't want me."

"What?"

"I keep asking her out, and she keeps turning me down. *Fuck.* I'm worse than Nate."

"No way, dude. He's not her mate. *You* are. Dammit!" Jason propped him up and gave his shoulders a squeeze, like a coach prepping a fighter for the ring. "Go out there and get her. You're a Lennox. A dragon, for God's sake."

"You know what, you're right." He straightened his shoulders and marched behind the bar, ignoring Tim's protests as he yanked open the door to the back room.

"Fucking rich boy shifters," Catherine muttered to herself as she kicked the door to the back room shut. Oh she knew his type well. Throwing around their money, thinking they could buy anything and anyone. It was one of the reasons she hated her old life and had taken off for LA. Controlling rich men who thought they owned you.

And what was that weird thing about being twins? Were they fraternal twins, maybe? Jason and Matthew looked like distant relatives. Sure, they were the same height and had the same large frame, but Jason's hair wasn't as dark and it was much thinner, and his nose was just a bit too big for his face. His eyes were also too close together, and now that she'd seen them side by side, Jason's were a dull gray instead of bright silver.

She leaned against the wall, trying to calm herself. Was she overreacting? Why the hell did Matthew Lennox get under her skin so much? He was just a guy. She wasn't some teenager pumped with hormones seeing her first crush. So what if Matthew Lennox was a tall drink of water on a hot day? It would never work out between them. He was a billionaire dragon CEO and she was ... what? She was going to be leaving as soon as she had enough money, that's *what*.

She was just in Blackstone to lay low for a while until she threw the Brotherhood's scent off. And getting involved with the biggest apex predator in the world was certainly *not* laying low.

The door to the storage room flew open. "I'm not done with my break, Tim," she said in an annoyed voice. But the shadow in the doorway was definitely not Tim. The hairs on the back of her neck bristled, and she recognized the man standing in the doorway.

"Excuse me, this is for employees only! Can't you read the sign outside?"

Matthew strode toward her, his shoulders straight and back stiff. The air around her suddenly felt cold and thin as power rolled off of him. It was too much, and she backed away. He didn't stop, just kept walking toward her until he trapped her against the wall, hands planted on either side of her. Before she could protest, he lowered his mouth to hers.

Catherine stiffened, and time slowed down as their lips touched. His mouth was surprisingly soft, but his kiss was urgent. Hot desire curled out from her middle, spreading through her body as he moved his lips against hers in a slow dance that left her breathless. Her knees buckled, and, to steady herself, she grabbed onto his shoulders.

His lips coaxed hers, parting them so he could taste her. He was like a man dying of thirst, drinking from her like she was the only oasis in the desert. His mouth—*God, his mouth*—owned not only her lips but all of her. She was burning hot from the inside. Was this what it was like to kiss a dragon shifter? Or was it just Matthew?

Rough fingers brushed at the skin on her neck and moved up into her hair, curling around the locks. He pulled gently at her scalp, and desire shot straight to her core, making her groan. His mouth moved lower, and while she whimpered at the loss, she soon let out a gasp when his lips pressed against her neck.

"Matthew," she whispered, lowering her eyes. His body was so close to hers, not touching, yet she could feel the warmth and power from him.

He pulled away from her, but braced his hands on the wall behind her again. "We're going out."

"Huh?"

"You. Me. On a date. When are you off next?"

"Uh, tomorrow?" Wait, was he asking her out?

"Okay then, I'll pick you up at seven."

Wait, he wasn't asking. He was *telling* her. "You can't—"

He cut her off with another kiss. "Don't be late." With that, he turned around and strode out the door.

"What the …" She blinked. She was going out on a date with Matthew Lennox. "*Sonofabitch.*"

CHAPTER 6

MATTHEW FELT PRETTY proud of himself as he left the office at 6:45 pm on the dot. With focus and determination, he had finished all his work by six p.m., got showered and dressed in his private office bathroom (thank you, Mom, for that luxury), and then was on his way to pick up Catherine. Hopefully, she'd be ready because he sure wasn't taking no for an answer. Not after that kiss. The memory of it would be forever burned in his mind.

To say he'd never felt like this before was an understatement. Sure, he'd had his share of women, but he'd always kept himself at a distance, never dating anyone seriously. He was just too busy, too focused on the future. Sex was a biological need, an itch he needed to scratch.

But with Catherine ... this was it. She was his mate. And how he was going to tell her and make her his was going to be difficult. She was human. She didn't understand how fast it was for shifters, how, when their animals chose, that was it. No one else would do, not from this point on.

He had to make it work. He figured it all out in his head.

Dinner at Giorgio's, the Italian restaurant in town. Then maybe dessert and coffee at Rosie's. Matthew planned to be the perfect gentleman tonight, just to make sure she didn't have any objections. *Take it slow*, he told himself. Hell, he'd be glacial if that's what it took to win her.

Matthew arrived outside Catherine's apartment building and parked in front of the hardware store. He got out of the car, strode to her front door, and pressed the doorbell. He waited for a few moments, then the silence from the other side made him start to wonder if she'd changed her mind.

Footsteps and the jingling of the doorknob made him straighten his shoulders. The door opened, and Catherine peeked out from behind it. With a long sigh, she pushed it wider and stepped out.

"You didn't tell me where we're going," she said as she locked the door behind her. "I hope it's not anywhere fancy because this is the fanciest thing I own." She gestured to her outfit.

Matthew stifled a groan. The sweater dress not only made her eyes bluer but clung to her delicious curves. And those knee-high boots over her leggings looked incredibly sexy. He wondered if they would be difficult to take off. "It's ... good. It's just a casual Italian restaurant."

She nodded. "Fine. Let's go."

Matthew tried not to let her flippancy get to him, but it was maddening to want someone so much and to have them treat you so coldly. Where was the Catherine from last night? The one who responded to his kisses eagerly. He'd even prefer if she resisted and fought him like she did when she was at the bar. He shook his head mentally. Was this the way he had treated the women who hopped in and out of his bed?

Someone out there was probably laughing at the karmic justice.

He led her to his Range Rover, opened the door for her, and helped her inside before he went to the driver's side.

Giorgio's Restaurant was right on Main Street in Downtown Blackstone. The restaurant itself was older than him, as far as Matthew could tell, and the owner, Giorgio, was a good friend of the family's.

"Matthew Lennox! What a surprise," Giorgio greeted as they entered. Matthew could remember coming here as a little boy for all their special family occasions, and the flamboyant owner looked the same as always—black hair perfectly coiffed, Italian-cut suit fitted to his slim figure, shiny black shoes polished to a mirror shine, and a warm smile. "I saw your name on the reservation list, and I thought you'd be here with your brother or sister." He looked at Catherine. "Not a gorgeous date."

Matthew laughed. "Giorgio, this is Catherine Archer. Catherine, this is Giorgio Allementari, owner of Giorgio's."

"Lovely to meet you."

"*Signorina*," Giorgio said with a deep bow. "You honor us with your presence."

"Uhm, thank you," she said with a sheepish grin.

"Now," Giorgio began as he took two leather-bound menus from the host's table, "I'll be attending to you personally tonight. And I have your usual table, of course."

"Thank you."

Giorgio led them to a large, semi-circular booth in a cozy corner of the restaurant. He gestured to the seat, and Catherine scooted in, placing herself on the farthest end while Matthew remained on the other side. Giorgio handed them the menus and excused himself.

"Your usual table, huh?" Catherine said without looking at him, her eyes fixed on the open menu in front of her.

"*Family* table," he corrected. Did he detect a hint of jealousy? Maybe she wasn't as indifferent as he'd thought. "We've been dining here since I was born." His father called it his "lucky" table, and it was only when he and his siblings were teens that the phrase made sense when Giorgio relayed the story of his parent's first date here. His mother blushed hard, while his father had a nostalgic (and slightly lecherous) smile on his face. Sybil refused to eat at the table for a year.

"Oh, so you know what's good," she said, putting the menu down.

"Did you want me to order?"

She shrugged. "Yeah, whatever. It's just food."

His irritation was growing. *Maybe you shouldn't have tricked her into going out*, a voice inside him said. He told the voice to shut up.

Thankfully, Giorgio came back with a bottle of wine. "Our best, as always, Matthew," he said with a flourish as he opened the cork and poured a small measure into a glass.

Matthew tasted the wine and nodded, then Giorgio poured them both a glass. "Giorgio, could you just send us the usual? You know my favorites."

"Of course, Matthew," he said with a bow, then turned to Catherine. "I'm sure the *signorina* will love all of it, as well."

"I'm sure I will," she said warmly. "Thank you."

The indifferent mask on her face slipped back on as soon as Giorgio left. She reached for her wine and took a sip. Her brows wrinkled as she swallowed.

"Good?" he asked.

"Surprisingly," she said, putting the glass down.

"What, you don't think this little backwater town has a good wine selection?"

"Ha. Blackstone is not a little 'backwater' town." She looked around, at the decor, at the rest of the diners. Everywhere except at him.

"Oh? Tell me, Catherine, where did you grow up? And why move here?"

Her eyes snapped back to him. For a moment, he saw a flash of something there … something not quite right. Apprehension. Fear. His dragon reared up, wanting to know why she reacted this way. "Well? Are you from Europe? Where did you live?"

"How did you …" She shook her head and grabbed the glass of wine again.

"Keen hearing," he said, tapping his ear. "You work hard at concealing your accent. I can tell. Or maybe you've spent a lot of time stateside so it's hardly there anymore. Were you born somewhere else? When did you move here?"

"It's none of your business," she said with a scowl.

Before she could say anything else, Giorgio came back. "Here you go. Our famous bread with our homemade vinaigrette." He put down a tray with bread and a small bowl with a dark liquid. "Enjoy. I'll be back with your antipasti."

The smell of the fresh-baked bread assaulted his senses, and Matthew couldn't resist. He grabbed a piece of bread, dipped it into the strawberry vinaigrette, and popped a piece into his mouth. Some of the oily liquid dribbled down his chin, and he licked it up. He realized that Catherine had been watching him, her eyes fixed on his lips and tongue. Finally, a reaction.

"Like what you see?" he asked.

"I don't know what you're talking about."

He scooted closer to her. She was already so far at the end of the bench, the only way she could get away was if she fell off. But she remained seated, her body suddenly going stiff. "Are you ever going to tell me any of your secrets?" he asked. Tentatively, he touched a finger to her cheek. "I want to know more about you, Catherine Archer."

"There's no secret, no mystery," she said, turning her head away.

He moved this finger down to her chin to tip her head back toward him. "I can't stop thinking about you. And about our kiss last night."

"Matthew ..." Her eyes dropped down to his lips again.

He couldn't stop himself. Nothing could stop him as he bent his head to touch his lips to hers in a tentative kiss. He didn't want to scare her since she already looked like she wanted to bolt. He took it slow, moving his mouth in a soft caress. When her lips parted slightly, he accepted the invitation and slipped his tongue into her mouth. She tasted like wine, and something else. Sweet and spicy, just like last night. Maybe this was a lucky table.

Someone clearing his throat made him pull away from her and slide back to his side of the booth. Catherine let out an adorable squeak of surprise. When he looked up, Matthew saw Giorgio standing by the table, a huge smile on his face.

"I brought you your antipasti platter," he said. Matthew was glad he was enough of a professional not to comment on their canoodling in his restaurant, but there was a twinkle in the old man's eye, one that seemed to say, "Way to go, Matthew!"

"Thank you, Giorgio. Catherine, I—" He frowned when he looked at her. "Catherine are you all right?"

"Huh?" She asked as she scratched her neck. "What's wrong?"

"Uh ... your face ..." A red, angry rash had suddenly appeared on her cheeks and neck, one that he was pretty sure wasn't there before he kissed her.

She opened her mouth and let out a choked gasp. Her eyes went wide, and she looked at Matthew and then down at the bread. "I ... I ..." She heaved and pointed at the bowl of vinaigrette. "What's in ..."

"It's our very own strawberry vinaigrette," Giorgio said. "What's wrong?"

Her mouth fell open. "Straw ..." She shook her head.

Matthew's heart dropped, and panic filled his veins as she began to take wheezy breaths. "Catherine! Are you allergic to strawberries?"

She managed a nod before her eyes closed and she slumped forward. He pushed the table away, sending it crashing into a nearby wall as he caught her in his arms.

"Call an ambulance!" he barked to Giorgio. "Wait ... never mind." He knew the fastest way to Blackstone Hospital. He picked her up and started running for the door.

Matthew had never driven so fast in his life. Hell, his dragon was ready to rip out of his skin to fly her to the hospital, but that probably would have taken too much time shifting back and forth. The Blackstone Hospital was only a few blocks away, and he drove like a madman, then carried her into the ER himself. When the nurse saw Catherine's state, she immediately took her in. He didn't want to leave her side, but the stern-faced nurse would not let him go with her into one of the procedure rooms.

The nurse did confirm it was the allergy that had sent her into anaphylactic shock. When he heard the news, the first thing he did was run to the bathroom and scrub his lips raw with that godawful soap they always seem to have in hospitals.

"Will she be all right, Doctor Perkins?" Matthew asked as soon as the doctor arrived in the waiting room.

"She'll be fine, Mr. Lennox," Dr. Perkins said. "It's a good thing you got here quickly. Anaphylaxis can be quite nasty. With such a severe allergy, she really shouldn't be walking around without an epi pen," Dr. Perkins said. "Did you check her purse for one?"

He shook his head. "She didn't have a purse on her, just her coat."

"Hmmm ... well, I'll write a prescription. Have her fill it immediately."

"Can I see her now?"

"Of course. We'll have to keep her overnight if she doesn't have anyone to watch over her. I'm afraid her eyes are still swollen shut." He shook his head. "It's not a pretty sight; I have to warn you. Did she not know she was allergic to strawberries?"

"Uh ... I'm not sure. She didn't say." He wanted to kick himself. It was the vinaigrette, of course, but she didn't have any of it. It was from the kiss.

Dr. Perkins led her to one of the rooms down the hall. "Ms. Archer," he said. "Mr. Lennox is here to see you." He grabbed the curtains and drew it back.

"What?" came a weak voice. "No, I—"

"Catherine," Matthew said as he walked closer. "Are you—what the hell are you doing?" He expected Catherine to be lying down on the hospital bed, but instead, there was a figure covered from head to toe in a blanket sitting up.

"Don't look at me!" a muffled voice from under the blanket said.

"Catherine, what's wrong?" He turned to the doctor. "You said she was fine."

"She is," Dr. Perkins said.

"I'm ... I look like a monster," Catherine cried. "Please, just go, Matthew."

Matthew sighed and walked around to the side of the bed. "Sweetheart ... you're not a monster."

"You don't know what I look like," she said. "It's awful. I haven't even seen myself, but I know it's bad."

"Hey ... c'mon now ..." He grabbed the blanket and tugged at it, but she was holding on tight. "Catherine, I could never think of you as a monster. Besides, I'm the one to blame for this."

There was a loud sigh from under the blanket, and then it slid away. Most of Catherine's face was swollen. Her eyes were thin slits, and her cheeks had puffed up like a chipmunk's. Matthew had always thought chipmunks were cute. "Hey, now," he said when she tried to put the blanket up over her head again. "It's okay. It's not that bad," he lied. Not that he cared what she looked like. He'd been scared shitless that she had nearly died. And because of him.

"You're such a liar, Matthew Lennox," she said with a pout, or at least Matthew thought it was a pout. It was hard to tell.

"Ms. Archer," Dr. Perkins began, "we're keeping you here overnight—"

"What? No!" she protested. "I don't have insurance or ... any money to pay for the stay."

"It's taken care of," Matthew said. It was his fault she was in here in the first place.

"You're not paying for me," she said in a serious voice.

"It's fine," Matthew insisted.

"I'll pay you back," Catherine said. "Every single penny. Just give me the bill."

Dr. Perkins cleared his throat. "As I was saying, unless you have family or friends to watch over you, we have to keep you here overnight."

"What? I'm fine. You gave me the shot."

"Yes, but you can't see, can you?" Dr. Perkins asked.

"Yes, I can!"

"Then how many fingers and I holding up?"

Catherine paused. "Uhm … two?"

Dr. Perkins shook his head. "I wasn't holding up any. Which means you're not fit to be alone. You could fall or hurt yourself. You can't even walk out of this hospital."

"But … I don't want to stay. I … I don't like hospitals." She crossed her arms over her chest. "And my hospital bill will probably balloon if I stay here one night."

"I'll take care of you," Matthew offered.

"I said—"

"No, I mean, I can stay with you. At home."

"No!" She shook her head. "Absolutely not."

"Then you'll have to stay here," Dr. Perkins said.

"I … I … Fine," she said with a sigh.

"Good. I'll process your discharge papers, and you can be on your way." Dr. Perkins nodded at Matthew and then left.

"So that you know," Matthew began. "Most of my first dates never end up in the ER."

"Most of them?"

"Just a few," he joked. He leaned against the bed and took her hand in his. "I'm sorry. About the kiss. I mean, I'm not sorry about *the kiss*, but for almost killing you."

She let out a short laugh. "The kiss of death. This is a first, even for me." She sighed. "I really will pay you back. All of it."

"Shhhh … don't worry about that. I'm just glad you're okay."

"And you don't have to stay at home with me. Just toss me into my bed, and you can leave. I'll be fine in the morning."

The image of tossing her into a bed crossed his mind, but she probably imagined it differently than he did. "Nuh-uh. Doctor's orders. What if you need help in the middle of the night?"

"I'll be fine," she said. "I'm used to being on my own."

Matthew frowned. Another layer added to the mystery that was Catherine Archer. Why was it the more time he spent with her, the less he seemed to know about her? But he wasn't deterred. He was going to peel back all those layers and know the real Catherine.

"I told you, I'm fine," Catherine said as Matthew helped her out of his Range Rover.

"And I told you, I'm still going to help you," Matthew countered. "Now c'mon, let's get you up to your apartment."

Catherine mumbled something under her breath, but let him walk her to the door. He had already fished her keys out of her coat in case she tried to get away (not that she could; her eyes were still swollen shut.) He opened the door to her apartment. "I—Oh." The door swung inward, and he realized there was a long staircase that led up to the second floor.

"What's wrong?" she asked.

"The stairs."

"Right." She squared her shoulders. "I'll hold onto the banister and then—hey! Put me down!"

Matthew hadn't bothered to ask because he was, frankly, tired of fighting her. So, he just picked her up and carried her in his arms as he climbed up the stairs. Despite his exhaustion, he couldn't help but notice how holding her like this felt right. His dragon agreed and rumbled in contentment, breathing in her distinct scent as he buried his nose in her hair. If she noticed, she didn't say anything.

"I ... ugh!" She grumbled as he put her down. "Next time, give me a warning if you're going to go caveman on me."

"But then it wouldn't be as fun, right?" he said with a grin. "Now, let's get you inside."

"I told you, I'm fine," she said. "You can go now."

"Oh, is that so?" He jingled her keys in front of her face. "Okay then, go ahead and let yourself in."

It took her two attempts to snatch the keys from his hand. Then, she turned around and began to fumble for the door.

Matthew let out a sigh. His mate was stubborn as an ox, but he had to admire her determination. "C'mon now." She didn't even bother to protest when he grabbed the keys and opened the door.

He went inside first, flipping the switch on the wall as he entered.

"I told you it's shitty," she said wryly.

"Uhm, it's ... cozy," he said.

"It's small."

The apartment was one room with a futon in the corner, a cabinet, a small coffee table, and an armchair. There was a door in the corner that Matthew assumed was the bathroom, while another doorway led into a kitchenette.

"As you can see, there's no chance I'll get lost in this

mansion," she said in a sarcastic tone. "I can find my way to the bed, so go ahead and let yourself out."

"Stop being stubborn and let me help you," he said. "Why don't I start by helping you get ready for bed?"

"Fine," she said.

He got down on one knee and helped her out of her boots. His fingers brushed her calves, and he smiled with satisfaction when she shivered visibly. After he put her shoes aside, he led her to the bathroom and put some toothpaste on her toothbrush. He left her alone since the bathroom was small enough and he wanted to give her some privacy.

Matthew looked around Catherine's bare apartment. He couldn't believe she lived here. But, then again, she was new in town, so she probably hadn't acquired a lot of stuff yet. His dragon was scratching at him, as if it was mad at him for letting her live here. *Well, what am I supposed to do? Move her into the castle?* The dragon huffed.

"I'm done," Catherine declared as the door opened. She had removed her socks and her leggings but kept her sweater dress on. He swallowed a gulp as he realized how thin the dress was. He could see the curve of her unbound breasts and her nipples through the fabric. "I just want to go to bed. I—" She stopped short. "You need to go."

"You're still blind."

"And there's ... no place for you to sleep!" she said, her face flushing.

"I'll take the chair." He gestured to the lone armchair in the corner, though she couldn't see him.

"You can't fit in that," she said.

"Then I can sleep on the bed with you." His dragon nodded in agreement.

"No! I ..." She turned even redder.

"Will you stop being stubborn and just let me help you?" Matthew said in an impatient tone. "Look, this is hard for me to admit, but I feel guilty as hell for what I did to you."

"It's not like you did it on purpose."

"I know, but still … you nearly died tonight. And I'm responsible. Will you just let me make it up to you? Then I won't bother you anymore."

Catherine's shoulders slumped. "Fine.

He guided her to the bed and pulled the covers back, then helped her in. "Good night, Catherine," he said as he pulled the covers over her. She murmured something, then turned on her side.

With one last look at her, Matthew settled himself in the armchair.

CHAPTER 7

THE SMELL of the hospital was distinct. Something she'd never forget in her life. They had been there for days, after all. Though it seemed much longer than that.

Mama is sick.

When is she coming home?

We don't know, Katerina. We don't know.

Please, Mama, get better.

That antiseptic smell was threatening to overwhelm her. She reached out, clawing out ... reaching for anything. Anything to get away from it.

"Catherine. Catherine!"

She let out a gasp. Stale air filled her lungs, but at least it wasn't *that* smell. It had been a while since she'd had that dream.

Strong arms wrapped around her, a familiar scent filled her nostrils. Her mind was still foggy, and she felt so warm and calm that she slipped back into a dreamless sleep.

It must have been hours later when she woke up. Her brain felt less muddled, and the memories came flooding back. Dinner with Matthew. That toe-curling kiss in the restaurant. Strawberries. Her hands instinctively went to her face. The swelling had gone down. She let out a sigh of relief. Arousal and desire had turned to fear when she felt her tongue swell and it became difficult to breathe. Then she passed out.

There was something heavy on her waist, and she was pressed up against something hard. A naked, hard chest and bare thighs. *Matthew?*

Catherine tried to scramble up and remove his arm, but his grip tightened and brought her closer to his warm body. God, he felt so good, and all she wanted to do was snuggle deeper against his chest. But she couldn't.

She had nearly backed out of their date, but something told her Matthew was not going to give up. So, she came up with a better plan: be surly and so disagreeable that he would regret asking her out. Why he unsettled her so much, she didn't know. And all those questions about her past ... he couldn't find out the truth.

"Why are you thinking so hard this early?" he asked, his voice low and raspy.

"I'm not thinking."

"I can imagine so many better things to do at this time in the morning."

She moved her head to look up at him. "Does that line work with all—" Oh, why did this infuriating man never let her finish her sentences? And why did she just let him kiss her whenever he wanted?

She moaned when he rolled his body over hers, careful not to crush her under his weight. But he pressed down with enough pressure so she could feel the heat of his body and the hardness between his legs against her thighs. Damn him and his delicious, skillful mouth. His kisses were like a drug shooting straight into her system.

"Matthew," she moaned in protest when he moved his mouth away from hers. His lips trailed a path lower, down her neck, nibbling at the soft skin there. She bucked up against him, and he moved a hand down to part her knees so he could settle himself between her legs.

"You're so delicious," he whispered against her neck. A hand moved under her sweater, and the rough pads of his fingers sent a shiver through her body as they skimmed up her heated skin to her bare breasts. His fingers teased her nipples into hardness, and she whimpered. "Let me taste more of you, please, Catherine," he said.

She moaned and nodded, and he moved his head down. His hands pushed her sweater over her breasts, allowing the cool air to hit her skin. When his wet, hot mouth encircled a nipple, she let out a soft cry and dug her nails into his thick hair. He suckled again, and his tongue licked at that nipple while his fingers tweaked and pinched the other one.

"Oh ... God ..." She gasped when his hips began to move, rubbing his hard cock against her core. His length brushed against her just right. The only thing between them was her panties and his boxers. It felt incredible. Her body tightened like a bow being strung, and she feared she would snap any moment.

A ringing sound, loud and insistent, broke through the haze of desire. Matthew let out a soft curse, and she whimpered in disappointment when his mouth left her. He scrambled to his knees and looked around for the source of the sound, then, with another curse, hopped off the futon to grab his discarded trousers from the floor.

Catherine sat up, crawling to the edge of the futon, and

pushed the sweater dress down to her knees. Oh God ... they had almost ... and she liked it. A lot. She wanted him bad, as much as he wanted her, as evidenced by his cock which was threatening to break through the fabric of his boxers even now as he angrily tapped the screen of his phone. She covered her face with her hands, which were still hot with embarrassment.

"Yeah ... I know ..." Matthew said as he spoke into his phone and slipped his trousers on. "Sorry, I had an emergency at the hospital. No, I'm fine. I'll be there in twenty." With a long, drawn-out breath, he put the phone down and slipped it back into his pocket, then picked up his shirt.

"Catherine," he began as he sat back down on the futon. He reached out and touched her cheek. "How are you feeling? You look much better now."

"I'm fine," she said, trying to keep her voice even, though the touch of his fingers practically made her melt into a puddle. Or want to jump his bones. She gripped the bottom of her sweater to stop her fingers from reaching out.

"I'm sorry, I have to go. I didn't let the office know I'd be in late."

She glanced at the clock. Eight-fifteen. Well, he was CEO. Probably started his day at six in the morning. She nodded, unsure what to say. What was he sorry about? Sorry about the kiss (and more)? About the date?

He leaned forward and pressed a gentle kiss on her forehead. "I'll see you later."

She watched him stand, button up his shirt, and head for the door. When she heard his heavy footsteps fade away and the front door closing, she grabbed a pillow and buried her face in it. *Oh, God*. Did that really happen? Why didn't she resist and stop him?

Because she wanted him, too. It felt so right, and if it wasn't for that phone call, she knew it would have gone further. She was still wet, her body aching for him. She pressed her thighs together, feeling some relief at the pressure.

"No," she said aloud and got to her feet. She couldn't let this go on. She'd have to tell Matthew this would never happen again. She'd be more hardened in her resolve and avoid being alone with him from now on.

The great thing about working nights was that she had the rest of the day to run her errands or lay around in bed doing nothing. She usually did the latter, but today, all her mind and her traitor of a body wanted to do was think about Matthew. His lips ... his body and the muscles under his taut skin. Hard and well-developed.

Determined to get him out of her mind, she got dressed, left her apartment, and walked to Main Street where all the shops and cafes were located. Except for a quick trip to refuel on caffeine the first day she had arrived in Blackstone, she had never stepped foot there.

It was a cool, brisk day and Catherine hugged her coat closer. Blackstone was so different from where she grew up. For one thing, she was still getting used to this weather. If she told people the truth, about her childhood, they'd probably think it was paradise. It was, and it was days like this she missed the sparkling sapphire blue waters and the white sand and—

Something made her stop in her tracks. The hairs on the back of her neck stood straight up. She had been on the run long enough to know when she was being watched. Her stomach churned, and she pivoted, her heart thudding against her ribcage. The street was empty except for a car parked across the street and a couple of people—a teenage boy and girl walking hand-in-hand, a mother and child exiting the toy store, an elderly man sitting on a bench—but none of them had been paying particular attention to her.

Catherine walked away, picking up her pace as she turned a corner. She wasn't wrong. She was never wrong. There was someone watching her, she felt it. But who? Had the Brotherhood found her? Or someone else? She would have to be careful now and not attract attention. Maybe even get ready to bolt. *Shit.* She didn't have enough money for a cheap car, only a bus ticket. Even if she did, in this weather, a clunker probably wouldn't get her very far. Not to mention, something about Blackstone made her want to stay. It felt like the right place. She shook her head mentally. No, she didn't just think that. This place could never be home.

She checked her watch. It was early for work, but that only meant she could take her time. Maybe even walk in circles in case she had a tail. If she was early enough, she could also take her time eating her employee meal.

It took her an hour to walk to The Den. She circled Main Street a few times, walked in and out of several shops. The feeling in her gut never left. Soon, her shift started, and she was once again slinging drinks and opening bottles. But it was hard to get into her Zen space tonight with her mind so jumbled. Good thing it was slow, and she didn't mess up any orders.

Another thing was niggling at the back of her mind. Matthew Lennox. He said "see you later" when he had left this morning but didn't specify what that meant. Was he going to stop by the bar? By her house? They didn't exchange numbers, so she knew he wasn't going to call.

The night wore on, and there was no sign of Matthew. Maybe he wasn't going to come. She tried not to feel annoyed.

"Excuse me."

Catherine whipped around at the sound of the unfamiliar voice. A man had slid onto one of the stools and folded his hands over the bar, then looked at her with dark eyes. Her senses went tingling. *Shifter.* But this was a shifter bar, so that wasn't unusual.

"What can I get you?" she asked as she observed him. He was not too tall, slim, probably in his mid-forties. His hair was dark and thinning and clung to his scalp. There was something about him that didn't feel like he belonged here. Though she hadn't been in Blackstone long, she was a good observer. She knew the clientele here, and this man definitely wasn't the usual type that patronized The Den. The fabric of his shirt was too thin and fine, not the typical thick, practical flannel or denim most people wore. And his hands were smooth like he'd never done a day of labor in his life.

"Just a beer. Whatever you have on tap," he said, flashing her a grin.

"Sure." She turned and grabbed a mug from behind the bar, then filled it from the tap.

"Thanks, sweetheart," he said as she lowered the mug in front of him.

She turned to walk away, but a hand on her arm made her stop. The touch gave her goosebumps, and not the good kind.

"Hey, where are you going? You can chat for a minute, right?" His smile made her insides turn.

She pulled her arm away. "I'm sorry, sir, I have work to do."

"There aren't a lot of people here," he countered.

"There's work in the back that I need to get to. Excuse me, sir."

"You look familiar. Have we met before?

The words sent a chill through her. "No, I don't think so."

"C'mon now," he said with a leer. "Pretty girl like you, I'd remember you."

"I'm new in town, so, no, you've probably never seen me before."

"Is everything all right?"

Catherine whipped around at the sound of the gruff voice. *Tim.* He was standing right behind her, arms over his massive chest, eyes narrowed at the man. *Thank God.* "Sorry boss, I promise this is the last time I'll dilly-dally. Sorry sir," she said to the man. "I need to get to work." Tim didn't stop her, and she didn't want to explain further.

Her heart was still pounding as she went to the storage room in the back. Who was that man? Why did he think he'd seen her before? She had a bad feeling about him.

Another thought dug its way into her brain. Still no sign of Matthew. For some reason, all she could think about was his embrace—his strong arms around her and his warmth, as if it were the only thing that could ward the chill from her body. It was annoying because she had already told herself she was going to stay away from him.

With a long sigh, she wiped her hands on her jeans and turned around to leave the room. She couldn't hide in here forever; she'd have to go out eventually. When she reached the bar, she felt the tightness in her chest disappear as there was no sign of the creepy man.

The rest of her shift went by quickly, and soon she was saying goodbye to Tim, Heather, and the rest of her fellow employees. She zipped up her puffy jacket and trudged out of The Den.

"Hey, you!" someone called as she was barely two feet away from the door.

The voice made her stop. *No. Not him.* She should ignore him and run home. *Shit.* Then he would find out where she lived.

"What do you want?" she asked, pivoting to face him.

"What? I can't say hi to a pretty lady?" he asked, his lips curling up into a cruel smile. Coal black eyes looked back at her. "Now, it's really bothering me, but I feel like I've seen you before. You worked as a bartender somewhere else … out west."

"You must have mistaken me for someone else," she said quickly.

"Are you sure?" He stepped closer and reached out to touch her arm.

"Stay away from me!" she hissed. "Or I'll scream."

"Now why would you do a thing like that? I'm only being—"

"Is there a problem here?"

Relief flooded through her. She didn't recognize the voice but didn't care. She turned her head.

The man standing behind her looked familiar. He was tall, with long, blond hair cascading down his broad shoulders, and a thick beard covering half his face. His eyes were a golden color, and, for a second, she could have sworn they glowed.

"No problem," the dark-haired man said, and he dropped his hand to his sides. "I was just talking to the lady."

"Looks to me like you were trying to touch her." He sniffed the air. "*Dog.*"

The man didn't move, but Catherine could see the anger in his eyes. "I'm a hyena, you stupid lion," he growled.

"I know. Now, get out of here," the blond man roared. "And I better not see your face in Blackstone again or I'm going to tear your hide away from your body."

"You—" He froze. Behind him, the door opened, and a group of people walked out. There were two couples. Catherine recognized them as they had ordered their drinks directly from her. All four watched them, their eyes fixed on the two men.

The hyena shifter said nothing, but he flashed a menacing grin at Catherine. He walked toward the parking lot and got into a car near the end. She shivered, realizing it was the same car that had been parked on Main Street that afternoon.

"You don't got nothing better to do?" the blond man groused at the bystanders. The four of them quickly walked away like scared rabbits.

"You all right?" the blond man said when they were alone.

"Me? Yeah, I'm fine." Her eyes widened in surprise as she recognized who he was. "You're …"

"Luke," he supplied.

"You're … Matthew and Jason's brother," she said.

"I'm not their brother," he said quickly. "But Matthew did ask me if I could watch out for you and walk you home while he's stuck at work."

"At this hour?" she said, then slapped her hand over her mouth. "I mean … whatever, I don't care. And I'm fine, walking home alone."

"You didn't look fine, back there," Luke said. "Who was that man? Do you know him?"

"No," she said. "He's just some customer." She tried to sound casual. "Some guys you know just because they're big tippers. They think you owe them something. Well, good night." Without another word, she ambled toward her apartment. Her mind was filled with all sorts of questions. Who was that man? He was a hyena shifter apparently. The Brotherhood couldn't have sent him, right?

"I said I was going to walk you home." Luke seemingly had appeared out of nowhere and was now in front of her.

"*Christ on a cracker.*" She nearly jumped out of her skin. For a large man, Luke made no sound, even on a quiet winter night.

"I live right across the street," she said. "So you needn't bother." Luke let out a snort and said nothing, but kept walking beside her. Catherine sighed in defeat. "Fine." They crossed the street, Luke switching sides halfway, and then they arrived at her front door. "We're here, okay?" She slipped her key in the door and didn't bother to look behind or say goodbye.

She supposed it was rude, but she'd had just about enough of shifters for today. Sure, Luke didn't scare her as much as the hyena did, but there was just something about him that made her uneasy, too.

As she started up the stairs, a knock behind her startled her. "Ugh," she groaned as she walked back down. "Now what do you—Matthew?"

Silver eyes glinted up at her, and Matthew's handsome face broke into a smile. "Hello, sweetheart," he said. "Sorry about running out this morning. I was already at the office when I realized I didn't even have your number. Then I got stuck in a couple of meetings, and I had to do a teleconference with Hong Kong."

"Where's Luke?" she asked.

"He's around," he said. "Are you going to invite me in?"

"So you couldn't bother to come see me, and you sent your *brother* to watch over me?" she asked.

He frowned. "I told you, I couldn't get away."

"Right," she said with a huff.

"Did Luke say anything to you?" He moved forward and raised his hand, but she shrugged him off. "What's the matter?"

"Nothing," she said, flinching away from him. "It's just … I'm tired, Matthew. It's been a long day."

"I know," he said. "I don't want … I mean, can I just come in? We don't have to do anything."

"What do you want from me, Matthew?" she asked point blank.

He frowned. "I just want to spend time with you."

"Like this morning?"

"Yeah, of course, and—"

"Look, I know you're feeling guilty about last night, but it's okay." She held up a hand when he tried to speak. "And also, I might have to leave Blackstone soon."

"What do you mean—"

She gave him the first excuse that popped into her head. "My grandma's sick." She mentally crossed her fingers. "I heard … from my cousin. No one else can take care of her, so I'm going to go see her." The lie was like a heavy stone in the pit of her stomach, sinking lower and lower with each second.

"When will you be back?"

She shrugged. "Who knows … it might take her a while to recover."

The look on Matthew's face made her heart wrench. It was too much. She had to get away from him before she changed her mind. "So … I guess I'll see you around." Before he could say anything else, she slammed the door in his face. She bit her lip, and it took all her strength not to open the door again. She forced her body to turn and march up the stairs, each step making her body feel heavier and heavier.

As soon as she was inside her apartment, she shut the door and leaned against it. It was better this way. Tonight was a sign. Whether or not the Chesnovak Brotherhood had sent the hyena to find her, she'd been recognized. He knew that she tended bar out in L.A., and word could get back to the Pride. It was best she put as much distance between her and Blackstone as soon as possible.

CHAPTER 8

IT WAS JUST HER DUMB, stupid luck that there were no buses out of Blackstone the next day, nowhere going far away anyway. Most of them stopped in the next towns, but she'd have to wait overnight for the long-distance buses. That would mean spending money on a motel or spending the night at the bus station. Neither sounded appealing, so Catherine decided one more day wouldn't make a difference. The first bus the next day would take her to Georgia, which she had heard was nice this time of year. Not that she cared. As long as it was far, far away from here, it would do.

Catherine supposed it wouldn't be too bad. The sick grandmother story was a good cover, and it allowed her to give a day's notice to Tim and earn another night of tips. After tonight, she'd pack her bags and never look back, although she hated lying to her boss, especially since he'd been so good to her.

But she had no choice. Anything she touched, anyone she cared about would be destroyed by the Chesnovak Brotherhood. They would stop at nothing to keep her quiet.

Throughout her shift, her thoughts kept straying to Matthew. She hadn't forgotten the look on his face before she shut the door. Like … what? Heartbroken? She bit out a laugh. The man hardly knew her. He'd forget about her, move on, and have another gorgeous woman on his arm going to some fabulous gala next week. The thought of Matthew with another woman sent her stomach clenching, but she pushed that feeling away. This was about survival. She had to put him and Blackstone behind her.

She went home exhausted, and all she wanted to do was sleep. She packed her meager belongings into a bag before collapsing in bed. She dreamed of lions chasing after her in the savannah. And of Rissa. Poor Rissa, lying on the floor of the apartment, her blood staining the carpet they had salvaged from a dumpster just the week before.

It was a good thing she had the presence of mind to set her alarm after work. She woke up, got showered and dressed, then picked up her bag and trudged out of the apartment and down the stairs. The walk to the bus station would be about an hour, and she wanted to give herself extra time just in case.

When she opened the door, she started as she bumped into a tall, imposing figure. Looking forward, she first saw a brown uniform shirt with a silver star pinned to the chest. She moved her gaze up and a stern face under a wide-brim hat was looking down at her.

"Catherine Archer?"

"Yes?"

"I'm Police Chief Meacham," he said, his voice gravelly and rough. The man was older, his face weather-beaten, but his green eyes were sharp as an eagle's.

"What can I do for you, Chief?" she asked.

Piercing green eyes narrowed at her. "Are you leaving town?"

Catherine mustered every bit of courage she had. "Yeah. Uhm ... I have to take care of my sick grandmother back north," she said. "If you excuse me ..."

Meacham grabbed her arm, gently but with a firm grip. "I'm afraid I can't let you leave yet, Ms. Archer."

"Chief," she began. "What's this about?"

"Ms. Archer, do you know a Jack Cunningham?"

"Who?" she asked in a puzzled voice. She'd never even heard of that name.

"Are you sure?" he asked. "I'll give you another chance."

"Chief Meacham, can we skip the twenty questions please? I've got a long walk to the bus station. Now tell me what this is about."

"You're a person of interest in a case, and you'll have to come down to the station with me."

Catherine let out a frustrated sigh. "What for? What case? Tell me, and I'll do my best to help you, but I can't miss my bus."

"It's murder case, Ms. Archer," he said in a grim voice. "So, if you'd like to cooperate, I suggest you get in," he gestured to his police car, "and we can talk at the station."

"And if I don't?" she challenged.

"Then I'll have to upgrade your status to possible suspect and detain you."

She swallowed a gulp. "Fine."

"Thank you," he said. "Come this way please."

Catherine followed Chief Meacham to his car. After she got in, she sat with her back ramrod straight. This was a mistake. She didn't know a Jack Cunningham. It must have been a mix-up. *Shit.* She was definitely going to miss her bus unless she got a ride to the station. Maybe when he realized he had the wrong person, Meacham could have someone take her there.

The drive to the police station seemed agonizingly slow, though, in reality, it must have only taken fifteen minutes. The Blackstone P.D. headquarters was located in the middle of town. Meacham cut the engine, opened her door, then helped her out. He led her inside, past the front desk, and toward the back. As they walked through the bullpen, she saw the back of a familiar figure seated in front of one of the desks. It was hard not to notice Luke's imposing size, after all. But what was he doing here?

Meacham led her through a door. "Let's go into one of our interview rooms. It'll be more comfortable."

"Right," she huffed. This was no interview room. This was an interrogation room. But she was still convinced there was a mix-up, so she sat on the chair opposite of Meacham.

"So," the Police Chief began, "you said you didn't know Jack Cunningham."

"Correct," she replied.

Meacham reached for the tablet PC on the table and turned it on. He laid it on the table, turned it and pushed it toward her. "This is Jack Cunningham."

Catherine let out an involuntary gasp. *The hyena shifter.* But this wasn't an ordinary photo. Cunningham was lying on a carpeted floor, his eyes closed, and a bullet between his eyes. "Now do you recognize him, Ms. Archer?"

"I ... I didn't know his name."

"Did you know him by any other name?"

She shook her head. "No. I didn't know him."

"Well, that's mighty strange, Ms. Archer." Meacham took the tablet back and then swiped a finger across it. He turned the screen back to her. "Because he seems to know *you*."

A cold fear gripped her, spreading ice in her veins. There were pictures of her tacked onto a wall. She recognized all these photos. They were taken from Rissa's scrapbook and their apartment. One was of her and Rissa, their heads bent together and their smiles bright. They had woken up extra early to hike up to the Hollywood sign to catch the sunrise. She remembered that photo had been displayed proudly on the wall of their living room.

"How ... I don't ..." *The Brotherhood.* Now there was no doubt who had sent Cunningham.

"You didn't know he was looking for you?" Meacham asked.

"No ... I ..." She took a deep breath. "He came into The Den—that's where I work—and he ordered a drink. When I left work, he was there outside, waiting for me. But he left."

"I know," Meacham said. "Four witnesses put you and Cunningham outside the bar sometime after one a.m. Along with Luke Lennox."

Luke! Was that why he was here? "Luke scared him away," she stated. "Cunningham was harassing me."

"According to the witnesses, Luke threatened his life."

"I ..." *Oh no.* This was her fault. Luke was going to get in trouble. She straightened her shoulders. "Cunningham was rude! I'm sure Luke wasn't literal in his threats."

"Tell me, Ms. Archer," Meacham said in a cool voice that sent another chill through her. "Where were you between one and five a.m. today?"

"Asleep, in my bed," she said. "Like I usually am."

"Do you have anyone who can corroborate your story? Friend? Boyfriend? Lover?"

She swallowed a gulp. "No."

"Then I'm afraid I'm going to have to keep you here for a while longer, Ms. Archer."

"Should I be calling a lawyer?"

CHAPTER 9

THE CAVERN WAS dark and damp, but the air inside was filled with electricity and anticipation. Matthew took one deep breath and then spewed out a stream of fire at the rocks. Large chunks came tumbling down as the dragon fire loosened the stones.

A long whistle rang through the cave. "All right, Matthew, you're done!" Ben shouted. "And let's get those rocks processed!"

As the workers began to scramble about, loading the chunks of blackstone into carts, Matthew let out a last puff of smoke before he began to shift back into his human form. He shrank down, the scales retracting back into his skin and his claws retreating into his hands. Soon, he stood on the cold floor of the cavern, fully naked.

Ben tossed him a pair of jeans and a T-shirt. "Here ya go, cuz," he said. "Everything okay?"

Matthew began to get dressed, slipping the jeans on. "Yeah. Why?"

"Nothing." Ben paused. "Well, you know you don't have to

do this. Jason usually does a couple of shifts a week so you can concentrate on running Lennox."

It was an open secret (at least in the town) of how blackstone was mined. Blackstone was the hardest material on earth and could only be found in these mountains, making it sought-after by many industries. Unfortunately, it was also encased in the second hardest material in the world, *nitride londaleite*. There was only one thing that could melt it without harming the blackstone: dragon fire.

Matthew and Jason's family had been mining it for generations, ever since their great-great-great-great grandfather Lucas Lennox won the mountains in a card game. It made the Lennoxes one of the richest shifter families in the world, at par with the original robber barons of the industrial age.

"I know," Matthew said. "But I thought Jason could use a break." Dragon fire wasn't inexhaustible, and they needed a few days in between to replenish. But the truth was Matthew needed this.

He was battling a maelstrom inside himself. He could at least give his dragon some release. It was furious at him and fought him at every turn. It had never been like this. Shifters and their animals weren't separate beings but more like two sides of a coin. He lived in harmony with his dragon. Except right now it was mad at him, as if blaming him for his mate's rejection.

And he didn't even know why she rejected him.

Catherine had been willing and warm that morning he left. He gave a silent curse. If only he didn't have so many responsibilities. If only he hadn't left. But what had changed her mind? Unsure of what to do, he gave her some space. Though it took every ounce of strength not to go to her, he left her alone.

"Matt! Ben!"

Matthew turned in the direction of the voice. "What is it, Nate?"

A severe expression marred their friend's face, a rarity for the normally happy-go-lucky wolf shifter. "It's Luke. I just got a call from the police station. He's in trouble."

"Luke?" Ben asked. "In trouble with the police?"

Matthew snorted. That was definitely not like Luke. His adopted brother never attracted trouble and always did his best to steer clear of it. "There's probably some mix-up."

"Right? That's what I'm thinking," Nate said with a shake of his head. "We should go and check out what's wrong."

"I'll keep things going here," Ben said, the ever reliable friend and employee. "You go and sort it out. And let me know what happens."

"Will do," Matthew said as he finished dressing. "C'mon Nate."

The drive to the police station took nearly an hour. The roads going down to Blackstone from the mines were slick and slippery this time of year. Matthew had this strange feeling crawling down the back of his neck, but he didn't know why. It was a good thing Nate, his expression cool as a cucumber, was driving them. Though Nate hardly had a serious bone in his body, he was always calm under pressure.

As soon as they arrived at the station, activity seemed to slow down and all eyes went to them. When he was growing up, the police station was a small, one-story building staffed by six officers. Blackstone P.D. wasn't as busy as those big city police departments, but with the growth of the town and more people coming in, there was enough action that they needed to expand the police force over the years. And, of course, when they needed funds to expand the headquarters and hire additional police officers, the Lennox family was more than willing to provide what they needed.

"Excuse me," Matthew said to the large, burly man dressed in blue at the front desk. "My brother called me and said he was being detained?"

The man straightened his shoulders. "Mr. Lennox," he greeted. "One of our detectives just finished interviewing your brother. You can head right in." He nodded to the door on the left.

Matthew thanked the officer and turned toward the direction he had nodded to. As he and Nate entered the bullpen, it wasn't hard to spot his brother.

"What's going on?" Matthew asked as they approached Luke. He was sitting in front of an empty desk, his shoulders hunched over.

Luke looked up at him, his expression grave. "It's not me you should be worried about," he said. "It's your mate."

"Catherine?" That feeling crawling down the back of his neck was now going on full alert. "What happened?" The other day, when he couldn't get away from the office and didn't have a way of contacting Catherine, he had asked Luke to go to The Den and make sure she was okay. He trusted Luke, after all, not just to make sure Catherine would get home safely but to keep silent as he tried to sort things out.

"A detective picked me up this morning, asked me to come for a 'friendly chat.'" Luke snorted. "There was this guy sniffing around Catherine that night you asked me to look out for her. Now he's dead, and they got witnesses who saw me and her talking to him."

"Guy?" Anger began to bubble in him. "What guy? You didn't tell me about a guy."

"Can it, Matt," Nate said, looking around them. "You're

making everyone uneasy."

Several pairs of eyes—most likely the shifters of Blackstone's finest—were on them. All the other shifters in the room could sense the coldness in the air as Matthew's dragon made its presence known.

"You didn't give me a chance," Luke shot back. "You were so hell-bent on getting the fuck outta there when she shut the door in your face that you didn't hear me calling you."

That was true. The moment Catherine rejected him, he wanted to get out of there. Leave her space and forget *her*. His fists clenched at his sides. "So, explain again. From the beginning."

"Like I said, this guy was bothering Catherine and I got rid of him. Apparently, he turned up dead this morning in his room at Shady Mountain Motel. Police somehow traced a connection to Catherine and found witnesses who saw me and her at The Den."

"They think you killed this guy?" Nate asked.

"Yeah. They asked me where I was between one and five this morning, and I told him where I always was. You know we got security tapes around the castle. I even ran into a couple of the rangers."

Though Luke didn't live at Blackstone Castle anymore, he still patrolled the area around it at night in his lion form. It was a habit he had picked up when they were growing up, when nightmares would prevent him from sleeping. Hank had encouraged it, and though Luke never said anything, Matthew suspected it was one way he coped with the trauma from his past.

"So," Luke continued, "Meacham came to talk to me. Said I wasn't a suspect, but asked me to stay for a bit. It's my fucking day off, but he's the police chief, so I couldn't say no. And I'm glad I did because I saw him bring her in here. Took her down to the interview rooms."

"*Fuck*." What the hell was going on here? Who was that man and what was his connection to Catherine?

"Matt." Nate nodded toward the hallway on the right. Meacham strode out, heading toward his office.

Matthew didn't wait another second and marched over. "Chief Meacham."

Meacham's thick, bushy white brows drew together. "Matthew? What are you doing here?" He glanced behind him. "Luke's free to go; we just want to make sure he's available for another interview, if needed."

"Where is she?" Matthew growled. "Where are you keeping her?"

"Excuse me?" Meacham said, his expression shifting and shoulders straightening.

"Catherine Archer." He nodded to the hallway. "You're keeping her here."

"I'm not at liberty to discuss an on-going investigation," Meacham said. "Now if you'll excuse me—"

"Please, Chief," Matthew began. "You know me. You know my family." Matthew had never used his family name to gain any favors or influence in the town, especially when it came to legal matters. His parents had always instilled in him and his siblings that being a Lennox was not a privilege; it was a responsibility. They were there to protect the town, not take advantage of their position. He'd never been tempted to use his power. Until now.

Meacham let out a long sigh, then looked around the room. "All right. As a courtesy to you, Mr. Lennox," he began, emphasizing his last name, "Ms. Archer is in interview room two. She's asked for a lawyer, and I'm about to call the public defender's office in Verona Mills."

"Don't bother," Matthew said. "She'll have the best lawyer in town. Mine." He turned to Nate. "Call Sorkin." Nate nodded and took his phone out of his pocket, then stepped away. "Are you charging her with anything?"

"Not at the moment; not while we're still gathering evidence."

"Then why have her here?"

"There's definitely a direct link between her and the victim. I'm sorry, Mr. Lennox, that's all I can say. Excuse me, I have to make a phone call." Meacham held a hand up before Matthew could ask anything else, and then he walked away.

"Sorkin will be here in fifteen," Nate said.

"Good."

True to his word, his lawyer arrived at the police station right on time. Dressed in an expensive pin-stripe suit and with his hair slicked back, Bradley Sorkin stuck out like a sore thumb in the police station. He was human but a shark in the courtroom, which is why Lennox Corp had him and his firm on retainer.

"I'll take care of this, Mr. Lennox," Sorkin said as he approached Matthew.

"She does not see the inside of a cell," Matthew said in a voice that was deadly serious. "Do what it takes."

The lawyer nodded and walked toward the interview rooms. However, he nearly ran into Meacham, who was holding Catherine by the elbow and leading her out.

Matthew's dragon roared and wanted to rip up anyone who touched her. He hung on to the last shreds of his control. Ignoring Meacham and Sorkin, he walked straight to his mate. "Catherine," he said, placing his hands on her shoulders.

Her face was pale, and her blue eyes widened when her gaze fixed on him.

"Matthew?" she asked. "What are you doing here?" Her cheeks went red as if she was embarrassed to see him.

"Where are you taking my client?" Sorkin asked Meacham.

"To a holding cell," Meacham answered.

"I'm her lawyer," Sorkin said. "Are you charging her with anything?"

Meacham cleared his throat. "Ms. Archer is still a person of interest in this case while we gather evidence," the chief said. "We're going to hold her overnight."

"Why?" Matthew asked. "She's not being charged."

"Mr. Lennox, when I came to talk to Ms. Archer this morning, she had her bags packed and a bus ticket in her pocket," Meacham said. "You can see why I can't let her go."

"This is ridiculous," Sorkin said. "Charge her or let her leave."

"As you know, I can hold her without charging her for twenty-four hours," Meacham said. "And up to forty-eight hours for a serious crime like murder."

Catherine let out a gasp. "You can't …"

Matthew could smell and feel the fear rolling off Catherine. Her face grew even paler "Release her to my custody," he said to Meacham. "I'll make sure she doesn't leave town."

Meacham shook his head. "Mr. Lennox, I can't do that."

"Please," Matthew said. "You know Blackstone Castle is like a fortress. She won't be able to leave without anyone knowing it. And I'll personally vouch for her. You can lock me up if she skips town."

"Do you know who my client is?" Sorkin asked.

Meacham hesitated, then looked at Catherine, then at

Matthew. "Fine. Just fill out the paperwork and make sure she doesn't leave your home."

"She won't be able to leave without me knowing it."

———

Shock had stunned Catherine into silence. First, it was when Meacham told her he was putting her in a holding cell until tomorrow. She couldn't blame him though. He did find her when she was about to leave town, and her pictures were in the dead man's motel room.

Then, as Meacham was taking her to the holding cell, seeing Matthew at the station had caught her off guard. Was he there for her? But why? No, she couldn't read more into this. He was there with his lawyer for Luke, and he saw her.

She glanced over at Matthew in the front passenger seat of Nate's truck. They dropped off Luke at his house and were now on their way to Matthew's home, where she would have to stay until they cleared her or arrested her. She supposed it was better than being in some holding cell at the police station, but she knew what it was: trading one prison for another. This one may be a gilded cage, but it was still a cage. And she already knew how it felt to be trapped in one.

"We're here," Matthew said as the truck slowed down.

Catherine glanced outside. What she saw silenced her again. Matthew had called his home Blackstone Castle, but she didn't think he meant a literal castle. Blackstone Castle stood on the side of the mountain, making it look even more majestic. Its tall spires and snow-topped towers seemed to reach up into the sky, and she almost expected knights to come rushing out to greet their lord or a princess to wave from one of the windows.

"Catherine?"

She had been staring up so long she didn't realize Matthew had opened her door. "I ..." Her eyes remained fixed on the castle even as she hopped out of the truck.

"Yeah, it's a castle," Nate said with a chuckle. "Well, I'll be seeing you. I need to get back to work." He waved to them, started the engine, then drove away.

"Welcome to my home," Matthew said, his voice soft.

"It's beautiful." It was breathtaking, especially against the clear blue winter skies. "You really live here?"

"Yes," Matthew said with a smile. "I grew up here with my parents and my siblings. Jason and Sybil prefer to live closer to town, though they still have their rooms here and sleep over every couple of days."

"And your parents?"

"Well, they retired recently and are on a round-the-world trip with their friends. They plan to be gone for at least a year and haven't decided what to do after the trip."

Matthew led her to the front of the castle, and the door opened. On the other side was an older man, probably in his early fifties, dressed in a cleanly-pressed white shirt and brown trousers.

"Matthew," the older man greeted. "Welcome home. I wasn't expecting you."

"I'm just here to drop off Ms. Archer. Catherine," he began, "this is our butler, Christopher."

"Nice to meet you, Christopher," she said.

"Likewise, Ms. Archer."

"Please, call me Catherine."

"She'll be staying with us for a while," Matthew said. "Please have the guest bedroom in the East wing prepared, and arrange for someone to pick up her things from her apartment. I'll text you the address." He turned to Catherine. "I'm sorry I have to go. I don't want to leave you alone again."

Her cheeks warmed, remembering the last time. "It's fine; I know you're busy."

"Anything you need, just ask Christopher or any of the staff. Or Meg, she's our housekeeper. You'll probably meet her soon enough."

He leaned down and gave her a soft kiss on the cheek. "We'll talk tonight. Everything will be fine. I'll take care of you."

And once again, Catherine was stunned into silence. Take care of her? What did he mean? She tried to dampen down the emotions threatening to burst inside her. All she could do was watch as Matthew strode away from her.

"Ms. Catherine?" Christopher asked. "If you could walk this way, please."

She nodded and followed Christopher inside. The castle was breathtaking on the outside, but it was even more beautiful on the inside. Whoever had designed it obviously had great taste. While they retained what she imagined were the original walls and detailing, they had modernized the interior, but their choice of furnishings, carpeting, and interior design elements still fit the castle theme.

"Is this castle very old?" she asked Christopher as they ascended the grand staircase.

"Lucas Lennox, Matthew's great-great-great-great grandfather, built it sometime after he founded Blackstone town and the mining company," Christopher explained. "When his company was expanding, he traveled to Europe and met a beautiful Swedish Countess. It's said he fell in love with her instantly and begged her to come back to America with him.

The Countess jokingly said she would if he built her a castle, and so he did."

Catherine smiled to herself. She supposed that was where Matthew got his persistence. "Did they marry?"

"Of course," Christopher said with a smile. He led her to the right and down a long hallway. "The castle was renovated sometime after Matthew and Jason were born. Their mother, Mrs. Riva, wanted to refresh it so it was more modern and comfortable, but also expand it so her children could have their own space if they chose to stay here. The entire East wing was converted into four separate apartments." They turned left, and he led her down a short hallway. "This is the guest bedroom. I always have it ready in case Nathan or Benjamin want to stay over. The staff recently changed the sheets and left out clean towels." He opened the door. "If you want anything else, I'd be happy to get it for you."

The room was bigger than her entire apartment over the hardware store. There was a queen-sized canopy bed in the middle, a sitting area in the corner with a love seat and a couch, plus a large flatscreen TV on one wall. The floor-to-ceiling windows opened up to a view of the mountains.

"It's fine, I'm sure."

"I'll have someone retrieve your things and bring them here," Christopher said. "Is there anything in particular you wanted, Ms. Catherine?"

"Please, just Catherine," she said. "All my stuff should be in a bag by my door." She fished her keys out of her coat pocket. "Here," she said, handing them to him.

"Are you hungry, Catherine?"

The last meal she had eaten was that morning's bowl of cereal. "I'm not hungry."

"Nevertheless, I'll have some refreshments brought to you.

But for now, I'll leave you so you can rest." He gestured to the phone next to the bed. "If you need anything, just pick up the phone. It'll ring straight to one of our staff." He gave her a curt nod and then left.

Catherine looked around her at the luxurious surroundings. A gilded cage indeed. It felt entirely too familiar. She shrugged and looked at the plush, comfy bed. She had gotten up pretty early that day and had spent most of the morning at the police station. She lay on the bed, intending only to close her eyes for a minute, but, when she woke up, she glanced at the clock on the nightstand and realized she'd been asleep for hours.

She sat up. Her brain was muddled, but it only took her seconds to remember the events of that morning. She was trapped. Again.

No, this wouldn't do. She had to find a way to escape. Maybe she could ask for help from her "contact" again, but that was too dangerous. There would be more questions this time, and if her contact found out why Catherine was in trouble, it would all be over.

C'mon, Catherine. Think. You're a smart girl. The past year on her own had taught her to be resourceful and to think on her feet. Surely there was a way out of this?

A soft knock interrupted her thoughts. "Come in," she called.

The door opened, and a woman walked in, carrying a tray. Catherine estimated she was probably in her late forties. Her brown hair was tied back into a neat bun, and she was dressed casually in slacks and a pretty, embroidered shirt. "Hello dear, I'm Meg," she said as she set the tray down on the coffee table in the sitting area.

"Oh." She quickly sat up. "I'm Catherine ... uh ...

Matthew's friend."

"Christopher told me about you," she said, her kind face lighting up with a smile. "You slept through lunch, so I thought I'd bring you something to eat. Just some light sandwiches, cookies, and tea."

"That's very kind of you, Meg." Her stomach was feeling empty, and she was dizzy from hunger.

"No problem at all," she said. "But please don't fill up, okay? Matthew called me and asked me to prepare my special roast lamb tonight for dinner. It's his favorite."

Her mouth watered at the thought of roast lamb. It had been too long since she'd had it. "Is there a special occasion?"

Meg laughed. "Matthew didn't say," she answered with a twinkle in her eye.

"Oh. I don't have anything to wear."

"We're not formal around here," Meg said. "Just wear whatever you like. It's just you and him for dinner. Now, I have to go, but do give us a ring if you need anything."

"Thank you, Meg."

With a final nod, Meg left, and Catherine sat down on the love seat. She reached for a sandwich and devoured it in two gulps. Cucumber sandwiches. Mama's favorite. A flood of memories came back, but she pushed them away. Why did everything here remind her of the past?

She ate one more sandwich and poured herself some tea. As she took a sip, she contemplated her future. She could only move forward, after all. But still, she had to put the pieces of the puzzle together. For the past few weeks, she had struggled not to think about what happened in L.A., but she knew the key was there.

It was evident that the Chesnovak Brotherhood had sent Jack Cunningham to find her. What was he? PI? Bounty

Hunter? The Brotherhood had many connections in the crime underworld, so it wouldn't be unlike them to hire a specialist to find her. They were also careful not to send one of their own. The members of the Pride tended to stick out, after all. Like many apex predator shifters, they were tall, well-built, and had that look in their eyes like they were always hunting. According to Rissa, they were all loosely related and the Chesnovaks had a distinct look. Mean, strong, and dumb. *Just like that idiot, Ivan.* If only Rissa hadn't fallen for that dumbass.

Ivan had done something, she could feel it. She always thought there was something about him that was untrustworthy. He had been gone for a couple of days, and Rissa had been worried because he wasn't answering her texts. It wasn't unusual for him to disappear for days, but usually, he'd tell Rissa if he was going away, if not where he was going.

Then, one night, when she came home after a late shift at the bar, they were there. Ivan's "brothers." The door being open should have clued her in, but she was too tired. Rissa probably left it open, she had thought. As soon as she got in, four sets of golden, feline eyes stared at her. Then there was a soft pop and thud. Rissa's body slumped over on the carpet.

She dropped everything and ran. Ran as fast as she could.

Catherine didn't even realize she was crying. She wiped the tears from her eyes and took a deep breath. She had to find a way out of this before the Brotherhood got to her and before they hurt any more people. Would they dare come into Blackstone? It wasn't like the town was closed off to outsiders.

Also, who killed Jack Cunningham? Was it connected to her and the Brotherhood or was it a complete coincidence? Surely, the police would find some evidence that she didn't do it. She'd watched enough police procedural shows to know they needed proof against her, even if she didn't have an alibi. He'd been shot, so they'd have to find the weapon and connect it to her. She had never fired a gun in her whole life.

Too many questions and not enough answers. The tea had gone stone cold by the time she decided she was done thinking. Her head hurt. Looking out, she saw the sun sinking in the distance. How she hated these short winter days. With a sigh, she got up, grabbed her bag, and went to the bathroom.

The shower and bath area were just as plush as the rest of the room. There was a separate glass shower in one corner and a small jacuzzi tub in the other. Fluffy towels were hanging on heated racks, and on the counter was a wide array of soaps, shampoos, lotions, and other amenities. Catherine decided a warm shower was in order, and she quickly whipped off her clothes and jumped into the enclosed glass stall.

She took her time, luxuriating in the hot shower and the fragrant soaps and shampoos. Stepping out of the enclosure, she toweled off and slipped on one of the fluffy robes hanging behind the door, then she walked out into the room.

"Jesus!" she cried out, nearly jumping out of her skin. The tall figure waiting by the window turned around.

"Sorry," Matthew said with a sheepish grin. "I knocked, and you didn't answer."

"It's fine," she said.

"Do you like the room?" he asked.

"Yeah, it's nice," she said. She hated to sound ungrateful, but she couldn't forget what she was here. A prisoner. "What are you doing home?"

"It's Friday night," he said. "I'm done for the day."

You and me both, she said silently. "I thought a CEO's work is never done?"

"It's not," he said with a chuckle. "But I gotta get home sometime or Meg'll send out an APB."

"Is it almost dinner time?"

"Yes," he said. "Unless you're not hungry? Meg says the lamb's almost ready."

The thought of lamb sent her mouth salivating again. "No, I'm good. I should … uh …" She looked down at her robe. "I should probably get dressed."

"Of course," he said with a nod. "I'll wait outside."

"Thank you."

As soon as the door closed on Matthew, she grabbed her clothes and put on her best sweater and jeans, blow-dried her hair, and put on some makeup. As she stared at her reflection, she wondered why she bothered to look nice. It was just dinner at home. Matthew did take responsibility for her, so he had to feed her too, right? With one last glance at her reflection, she walked to the door.

CHAPTER 10

CATHERINE DIDN'T KNOW what to expect at dinner. After all, they were in a castle. She had initially imagined they would be in some austere dining room at opposite ends of a long table. But no. Matthew led her into a small, cozy dining room just down the hall from where her room was. He explained this was the informal dining room for the East Wing. Dinner was laid out on the small cherry wood table in the middle. Meg had taken out the lamb when they sat down but informed them that she and Christopher were headed home for the night and that they would be on their own for dinner. Matthew explained that Christopher and Meg, like many of the staff, didn't live in the castle but rather in their own little cabin on the property.

Matthew served her some lamb; it was delicious. Different from how she usually had it, but it was perfectly cooked and tender. They also had dinner rolls, potatoes, and buttered vegetables to go with the meal, as well as wine. Catherine was stuffed by the end.

"Meg told me that she was leaving us dessert and a nightcap in the library," Matthew said.

"I can't eat another bite," she declared.

"Oh? How about a tour of the castle then? To help us digest?"

She nodded. "Sounds nice."

Matthew stood up and helped her out of the chair, then led her out of the dining room. "This is the newer wing of the castle," he explained. "Jason, Sybil, Luke, and I all have our own mini-apartments here."

"But they don't live here anymore?"

He shook his head. "They all moved away at some point. Jason likes being in the center of the action, so he got one of those fancy penthouses in the newer area of town. Sybil's kind of a workaholic, so it just made sense for her to have her own place near her office. Plus, she joked that she'd never find a boyfriend if she lived at home with her parents and siblings. Not that she has time."

"And Luke?"

He paused. "He prefers to live alone."

Catherine didn't press further but sensed that there was more to that story. Not that she'd be around long enough to find out. She'd already decided that the moment Chief Meacham declared she wasn't a suspect, she would leave Blackstone. There was a strange knot forming in the pit of her stomach, but she ignored it.

"So you mean to tell me, you live all alone in this huge castle?"

He laughed. "Yes, I guess so."

"Don't you feel lonely? What about your siblings? Don't they want to live here?"

"I guess I do feel lonely sometimes." He paused as they reached the staircase, then he led her down. "And, as for my siblings, they're always welcome here. But it's like ... it's difficult to explain, but let me try. There's always been a Lennox dragon living in Blackstone castle," he said. "I suppose as the oldest of my siblings, I've always felt responsible for taking care of it. Jason and Sybil don't mind. Sybil's always been independent, and she loves her job as a social worker. And Jason's happy with his life the way it is and has never wanted to be CEO. He prefers the easy life, working in the mines and at the foundation."

"So you're inheriting all the responsibilities, along with this castle."

"Something like that." They stopped when they reached the bottom of the stairs. "And the castle won't be empty all my life. I suppose someday it's going to have my children in it."

The tightness in her stomach grew and spread to her chest. Of course Matthew would have children someday. He needed someone to continue the line and pass all this on to.

"Anyway," Matthew said, clearing his throat. "I want to show you the older parts of the castle first. My mother supervised all the renovations, though my Aunt Laura, that's Ben's mom, helped a lot. They kept most of the original interiors ..."

Catherine pushed all thoughts of Matthew and his future children aside and listened to him as he guided her through the castle. It was actually quite interesting, and Matthew added a few stories about his childhood and growing up.

"Ready for dessert?" he asked as he led her into what she assumed was the library.

"Sure."

The library, as Matthew said, was one of the few rooms

that wasn't renovated. They had reupholstered the furniture and cleaned the carpets, but that was it. And Catherine could guess why. It was beautiful. Three walls were filled from top to bottom with rows and rows of leather-bound books, while a cozy reading area with comfortable-looking wingback chairs and a couch were set up in one end. A roaring fire was burning in the fireplace, bathing the room in a warm glow.

"Would you like dessert, coffee, or a drink?" Matthew asked.

She felt her mouth go dry. The glow of the firelight hit the angles of his face in just the right way, making him seem even more handsome. He had discarded his jacket long ago and the shirt he wore stretched deliciously over the muscles of his chest. His silvery eyes had that unearthly glow, and he looked at her with heat that sent desire straight to her core.

"Uhm, maybe one drink," she said.

Matthew gestured to the couch, and she sat down. "Is bourbon okay?" She nodded, and he poured some liquid from a decanter into a glass and handed it to her.

Catherine accepted it and took a sip. The amber liquid tasted smoky and left a warm path from her throat to her stomach when she swallowed. "Smooth," she said.

Matthew sat down next to her, his own glass in hand. "How are you feeling?" he asked, his voice serious. "I'm sorry about today."

"I suppose I should thank you." She shook her head. "No, I mean, thank you." She took another sip of the bourbon. *For courage.* "I don't mean to be ungrateful. And your home is beautiful."

"I'm glad you think so." He took a sip of his drink, then put the glass on the table. "Are you going to tell me who that man was? Why they think you had something to do with his murder?"

Her fingers gripped the glass so hard, her knuckles went white. "I ... can't." She didn't want to lie to Matthew. At this point, there were just too many lies and she feared she would drown in them.

"If someone's out to get you, just tell me. I can protect you," he said, his voice sincere.

He couldn't mean that. Sure, he was rich and powerful. Plus, a dragon. But this wasn't his fight. The consequences ... they would be too much, and the price to pay was too high. "Matthew ... please." *Please stop. Don't ask me to lie to you anymore.*

Matthew took her hands in his. "Catherine ... tell me you feel this, too." He placed her hands on his chest, and she could feel the beating of his heart. "I don't know how to say it because this must feel so fast for you, but for me it's been so slow."

"What are you saying? I don't understand." *But you can feel it too*, a voice said. Her hands shook slightly.

"I promise to protect you," he said, lifting her palm to his lips and kissing her pulse. "Whatever it is."

She moved her hands up to his face, touching him as if she were memorizing his features. She'd been running away for so long and denying herself. She was still determined to go once she was cleared. Surely, by tomorrow, Meacham would have found the real murderer or at least removed her from his suspect list. But, after everything she'd been through, why couldn't she throw caution to the wind for once? Just for tonight.

She closed her eyes and leaned forward. He met her halfway, and as their lips met in a fiery kiss, her heart threatened to burst from her chest.

His long, elegant fingers dug into her hair, scraping her scalp. When he tugged at her hair, she let out an involuntary moan, opening up her mouth and allowing him to slip his tongue inside. He tasted delicious, like the smoky bourbon plus something else. Hot and wet. Fierce and sweet at the same time.

"Matthew ..." she whispered as she pulled away. "Take me upstairs." He nodded and then swept her up into his arms.

It seemed ridiculous, being carried up to a tower in his castle, but somehow it made sense. She lay her head on his chest, listening to the beating of his heart. At first, she thought he would take her to the guest room, but she was surprised when they turned a different corner, and she realized they would be going to his room.

Catherine looked up at him as he placed her on top of his king-sized bed and brought his head down for another kiss. The duvet felt soft and silky underneath her, a contrast to the warm, hard planes of his body. She moved her hands up to his chest, feeling the muscles and reaching for the buttons on his shirt. Despite her nervousness, she somehow was able to get the buttons opened and ease down his shirt. His bare skin felt hot to the touch, like he was running a fever, and she wondered if that was because of his dragon.

Matthew's lips never left hers as he continued to suck and nibble and sip at her. His hands, however, roamed her body freely, cupping her breasts through her sweater and slipping underneath her to knead her buttocks and push her closer to him. She felt that hard press of his erect cock between her legs and found herself rubbing against him and mewling like a cat in heat.

"I need to feel you," he whispered as his hands dropped to the bottom of her sweater. Quickly, he slipped it over her head, revealing her thin, white bra. His silvery eyes burned with desire as he stared at her, his hands moving down to the front of her jeans as he popped the buttons and yanked them off. "You're so beautiful like this," he said, a hand slipping between her thighs.

"Matt—" She bit her lip as his fingers skimmed over her panties, the front of her pussy growing damp with each stroke. She squirmed, moving her hips in rhythm with his hand. Fingers pushed the white fabric aside, and he slid one digit into her wetness, making her clench around him.

"Come for me, Catherine," he urged as he bent his head lower, his lips capturing a nipple through her bra. The rough scratching of the fabric, now getting wet as it was enveloped by his mouth, felt deliciously wicked against her hardening nipples.

"I ... I ..."

"Just come, sweetheart. I'll be here."

He slipped another finger inside her and continued that maddening rhythm. She wasn't even sure how he did it, but the ripping of fabric told her he had torn her panties away. His thumb found her clit, and he stroked it until she arched her back and her hand fisted around sheets as she came.

He withdrew his fingers from her, and Catherine watched from under lowered lashes as he slipped his fingers into his mouth. "You're delicious. I need more," he growled as he pushed her legs apart.

"Matthew!" The touch of his lips and tongue on her was exquisite and even better than his fingers. He licked, suckled, and ate her like he was dying of hunger. His tongue ... oh

God, his tongue. She thought it was amazing on her mouth, but down there ...

She let out a cry as another orgasm built in her. Matthew was relentless as he brought her over the edge once more. Her breathing was ragged as she came down from her orgasm. It had never been like this, not for her.

Matthew moved away from her, standing up over the bed as he discarded his trousers and underwear in one motion. Even in the low light of his room, she could see his cock. It was thick, long, and stood erect and proud. For a moment, she thought about all those groupies who came to Blackstone just to sleep with shifters, and she lost all her judgment. That thing between his legs was definitely threatening her with a good fucking. Because this was all this was, right? Just one night of fucking.

She reached for him, and he let out a soft grunt as her fingers wrapped around his thick cock. The skin was velvety soft, but the shaft was hard. She gave a tentative squeeze and he twitched in her hand.

"I'm sorry, sweetheart ... you have to stop ... or else ..."

She let go, and he moved to the bed, kneeling beside her as he helped her take her bra off. His hands cupped her breasts, squeezing gently and rolling the nipples until she was moaning.

"Please, Matthew. Fuck me now."

He nodded and reached for the nightstand, withdrawing a silver packet. He tore the corner off with his teeth and then slipped the condom on his cock. Moving between her legs, he positioned his hips between her thighs and guided himself into her.

Catherine held her breath as he nudged into her. Slow, deliberate. He filled up every inch of her, and with each movement, she took more of him in, until he was all the way inside.

"Are you okay?"

She nodded.

He gave a short grunt, grabbed onto her calves and wrapped them around his waist, bringing him deeper into her. Catherine bucked up, the sensation too much. Then, he began to move. Short, small thrusts as her body adjusted to his. As she began to moan, he slipped his hands under her to pull her forward. More and more.

"Matthew!" Her hands grabbed onto his shoulders, and he pulled her up, so they were upright. He held onto her as he pushed back on his heels, her thighs around his hips. She moved forward, meeting his thrusts enthusiastically as the pressure began to build within her.

Matthew rolled them over until she was on top, straddling him as they clung together, face to face. His hand gripped the back of her head and pulled her down for a kiss as his hips continued to buck into her. She rode him, using the leverage of her knees to bounce up and down as his hands never left her head. They kept her in place as he continued to stare at her with those unearthly eyes. He watched her intently, moaning her name over and over again.

Her back arched, and she grasped the sheets with her fists as her body began to convulse. He kept going and going, fucking into her. She cried as pleasure tore through her body before collapsing on top of him. He kept going, giving a few final thrusts as he let out a grunt, and she felt his cock twitch and spasm inside her.

He groaned as he slowed down, then stopped. He gave her a slow kiss, his hands roaming over her sweat-slicked body. They lay still for a while, not saying a word. Finally, Matthew gently eased her off him as he rolled to his side and disposed of the condom.

This was just sex, Catherine reminded herself. She was glad now he had chosen to bring her to his room. It would have been awkward to ask him to leave the guest room since he technically owned it. Now she could simply put her clothes on and say good night. But, when she tried to scoot away, a hand snaked around her waist and Matthew brought her close to him. He brushed her hair aside and kissed her shoulder, then buried his nose in her hair.

"Matthew, I should—"

The soft snores coming from Matthew made her stop short. When she tried to wiggle away, his grip on her tightened. She let out a sigh. Maybe she could slip out later. Might be a better idea to wait, as she didn't know if any of the staff might be lurking about. She didn't want to be caught doing the walk of shame.

Catherine settled in, her body suddenly feeling tired. Her eyelids felt heavy, and she told herself she'd just close them for a short nap.

Catherine woke up hours later, while it was still dark. Matthew was sleeping soundly, his breathing even. As she tried to slip out of bed, he stirred, so she patted his arm reassuringly. He snorted, then rolled over. She breathed a sigh of relief.

She scrambled to the floor, feeling around for her jeans. When she found them, she took the small phone out of the pocket and began to type another coded message.

The weather in the mountains has turned, and I'm in the mood for a change. Somewhere warm and airy?

She pressed send and returned the phone to her pocket, then climbed back into bed. Matthew stirred again, then strong arms drew her in. He planted a sleepy kiss on her neck, then settled against her.

The sun wasn't out, so she probably still had a few hours. She could sneak in another quick nap before she had to go.

CHAPTER 11

Matthew couldn't remember the last time he had slept so deeply. Frankly, he was disappointed that he didn't wake up overnight. He wanted to make love to Catherine through the night and keep her up until she begged him to stop or passed out from an orgasm. However, he couldn't complain, not when her sweet, warm body was pushed up against him, and her golden hair was spread across his pillow.

He glanced toward the large bay windows and saw the light peeking from behind the trees and the mountains. He also couldn't remember the last time he had stayed in bed so late. Usually, by this time, he'd be up having his coffee and reading his emails. Of course, he'd never woken up in bed with his mate.

Mine.

His dragon snorted contentedly as he stared down at Catherine. Yes, she was finally his. However, other thoughts crept into this head. Jack Cunningham. She still refused to tell him how she knew the man, but he had seen the fear in her eyes. A million scenarios went through his head. He was a stalker. An ex-boyfriend. Or someone sent to find her. It had made sense. From what he has seen of her place and from what he could piece together, Catherine had rolled into town with nothing more than the clothes on her back. She was running away from something.

But that was done now. She would be done with running because Blackstone would be her home from now on. He had meant it when he said he would protect her.

"Wha …" Catherine stirred, her lids fluttering open. "I …" She let out a gasp, then sat up. "Oh my god. I overslept. I'm … my clothes!" She looked around, then scrambled up to her knees. She let out an indignant shriek when he grabbed her by the waist and pulled her against him. "Matthew!" The slender column of her neck lay exposed, and he couldn't help himself as he pressed his lips there, licking at the soft skin. She moaned and sank back against him.

"Hmmm … that's better," he said as his lips moved higher. He turned her head back toward him and kissed her soundly on the mouth. "Where do you think you're going and why would you need clothes?"

"Matthew …" she began, "it's late. I really shouldn't have stayed here." She stopped again when he planted his lips on hers. She let him kiss her again but pushed him away after a few seconds. "Your staff … Meg … they'll know."

"Know what?" *That I have my mate in my bed?*

"You *know*."

"No, tell me," he challenged. "Or maybe you could show me instead."

He didn't wait for her to say anything. Instead, he silenced her with a kiss and brought her hand down between his legs. His cock was already hard and throbbing, and while she hesitated for a moment, her warm fingers enveloped him again.

He moaned as Catherine's eager fingers stroked him, his hips moving in time with her hand. Her eyes were lowered, watching as his cock grew even harder in her grasp. God, he wanted to go on, but if she didn't stop, he'd come all over her fingers.

With a growl, he pulled away from her. She gasped in surprise as he pushed her back, then rolled her onto her stomach. "Let me worship you, Catherine," he said, covering her with his body.

He pushed her hair aside, revealing the smooth expanse of her back. He kissed the back of her neck, making her squirm and moan. Making his way down, he licked, kissed and sucked a path down her spine, dropping a kiss on the small of her back and then giving her ass a playful nip.

Matthew propped her up on her knees, exposing the full, pink lips of her pussy. She was already wet, the minx. Spreading her knees wider, he pressed his lips against her from behind.

"Matthew!" she cried, her head jerking back.

"You taste like heaven," he said, then licked at her again. Wetness gushed from her, dribbling onto his lips. He couldn't get enough. By the time he was done, she was writhing and squirming against the sheets.

He positioned himself behind her, his hands grabbing the creamy flesh of her ass. God, he'd been dreaming about this for so long, taking her like this. To let his primal side take over. He wanted nothing more than to slip inside her, fill her with his cum and get her pregnant with his child. His instinct was screaming at him to do it, but his more rational side prevailed. *Take it slow.* Matthew grabbed another condom from the nightstand and quickly put it on.

She let out one of her sexy little moans when he began to

push inside her. He hoped it wasn't too soon as she was still so tight around him. But he couldn't stop now. He could only make sure she enjoyed this as much as he did.

Placing a hand between her legs, he found her clit. He teased her, and he felt her tight passage get slicker with her juices. She whimpered and thrashed her fists on the mattress.

Fuck, she was amazing. Tight and hot and so eager, her body clenching around him with each thrust. He held her tighter, pulling her up so her back was against his chest. He grabbed onto her tits from behind, drawing her body down as he drilled up into her.

"Matthew!" God, even the sound of his name from her mouth made him hot. Especially when he was driving into her.

"Fuck, Catherine … I can't …" He felt her pussy tighten and squeeze his cock, her juices flowing down onto him. He let out a groan and let go, his orgasm tearing through his body like a hurricane. With one last thrust, he came, his knees buckling so bad he fell on top of her.

He rolled over before he could crush her, lying on his back as he stared up at the ceiling. Catherine was next to him, still sprawled on her stomach.

"So, what were you saying again?" he asked with a cheeky grin.

She turned her head and smirked at him, looking adorable with her cheeks pink from exhaustion. Her eyes turned stormy for a moment, and she let out a sigh. "Maybe I can still sneak out and get to my room. Before anyone finds out."

He sat up. "Catherine," he began as he traced his fingers down her back, "by now, the breakfast prepared by the staff will have gone cold. And Meg would have checked on you and realized you didn't sleep in the guest room. Cat's out of the bag, sweetheart."

She bit her lip. "I just don't want them to think …"

"That you came in here and ravaged me last night?" he asked, wiggling an eyebrow at her.

She laughed and hit him playfully on the shoulder, which prompted him to catch her wrist and pull her up so her arm sprawled across his chest and her face lay in the crook of his arm. "Catherine, we're two consenting adults. I don't think anyone is going to judge us."

"You mean me," she said.

He let out a sigh. "Catherine, I need to tell you—"

"You still in bed, old man?" a voice rang out as the door slammed open. "I thought you'd be up—" Jason's eyes went wide when his gaze landed on them.

Catherine let out a squeak and rolled off him, taking the sheet with her as she wrapped herself up like a burrito.

"Don't you ever knock, you asshole?" Matthew growled as he leaped to his feet. He didn't bother covering up; Jason had seen him naked countless times. Hell, Jason saw the same thing every day when he looked in the mirror.

"Sorry, bro," he said, putting his hands up in defense. When he tried to look around him, a possessive fury gripped Matthew and he pushed Jason, making him stagger back. No one would see his mate naked except for him. He grabbed Jason by the arm and dragged him to the door.

"I said I'm sorry," Jason complained as he yanked his hand away. "Though, I don't understand how you can be so grumpy when it's obvious you got your dick wet last night."

"Shut up!" He grabbed his brother by the collar.

"Fuck. Sorry. She's your mate; I shouldn't be talking like that."

Matthew let go of Jason and massaged the bridge of his nose. "It's fine. Sorry. I can't help it."

"Dude, you are so whipped." Jason slapped him on the shoulder. "I'm happy for you."

"Who's whipped?" A feminine voice echoed. "Jason, what's —*Oh my god!* Why are you naked, Matthew?" Sybil placed a hand over her eyes.

"For a shifter, you sure are a prude, Sybil," Jason said.

"Well excuse me for not wanting to see my brother's … thing!" she said. "What's going on? Were you out all night flying or something?"

"I guess you could call it flying—Ow! Goddammit, Matthew, you know I run my mouth sometimes. Fine, I'll stop."

"Then just stop talking and get the fuck away from me," Matthew warned.

"Will someone tell me what's going on?" Sybil said.

"Matthew spent the night with Catherine. His *mate*," Jason said.

"Your *what?*" she squealed. "You found your mate? And she's here?" Sybil looked ridiculous as she had one hand over her eyes, while the other was flapping around excitedly.

"Yep," Jason said, popping the p. "And she can tell us apart, too."

"Like what Mom said about Grandpa?" Sybil's voice pitched even higher.

"It's that Sinclair twin magic," Jason said.

"This is amazing!" Sybil screeched. "Oh my God, I can't wait to tell Mom and Dad! Where is she? Can I meet her?"

Matthew shook his head. "Guys, please. Sybil, stop hopping around; you're giving me a headache."

"I'm just so excited," she said.

"Could you guys …" He lowered his voice, in case Catherine could hear him. "She doesn't know."

"She doesn't know what?" Sybil asked.

"That we're mates," he said. "She's human, so she doesn't know about the whole mates thing."

"You need to tell her," Jason said.

"Look, it's complicated. There's a lot going on, and I'm trying to take things slow. We only met last week." Had it really only been last Saturday when he went to The Den? It felt like it had been forever ago.

"Fine, we'll let you go at your own pace," Sybil said.

"And no telling Mom and Dad, okay? Not yet." He glanced at Jason. "What are you guys doing here anyway?"

"Well, we know you just finished your first week as CEO of Lennox, so Sybil and I decided there was no way we were going to let you spend the entire Saturday working."

"You know Mom and Dad told us to make sure you're not working yourself into the ground, right?" Sybil said.

"So, we're here to take you sledding, like we used to do when we were kids," Jason stated. "We invited everyone, too."

"Of course, had we known you had other activities planned …"

Matthew shook his head. "Let me put on some pants so you can put your hands down, Sybil." He turned to go back into the room and closed the door behind him.

"Catherine?" he asked. The bed was empty, and there was no sign of her. "Where are you?"

The door to the bathroom squeaked open. "Is he gone?" Catherine asked as she stuck her head out.

"Jason's not in here anymore."

She let out a relieved sigh and trudged out of the bathroom, the sheet still draped around her.

"I'm sorry, sweetheart," he said, wrapping his arms around her. "Jason has zero boundaries. He's my twin, after all. We used to share everything."

"Right. Twins," she huffed. "What are we going to do now?"

"Well, I guess we're going sledding."

It had snowed overnight higher up in the mountains, which made it the perfect setting for a day of sledding. Catherine had seemed reluctant at first but was put at ease when she met Sybil. When Catherine said she didn't have any proper clothes for going out into the snow, his sister eagerly dragged his mate to her room so she could borrow an outfit. While he had been apprehensive at the thought of Catherine spending time with Jason and Sybil, he realized he had been worried about nothing. His more easy-going siblings knew how to put her at ease and make her feel welcome.

Soon, they were packing up the ATVs with their sleds, goodies from Meg for when they got hungry, and hot drinks packed into thermoses (as well as bottles of wine from the cellar.) They took three ATVs, and Catherine rode behind him, her arms around his waist. He thought she looked adorable in the pink parka and matching hat with her hair braided back. She thought she looked like a marshmallow, and the coat was a tad too big, but he didn't care. Pressed up against him like this, he could feel every curve of her body. It made the rest of the ride uncomfortable, and he was glad he was wearing a long coat to cover his hard-on.

When they got to their favorite sledding spot, which was a hill on the east side of the Lennox estate, they stopped and parked the ATVs. As their group began to unpack their things, the roar of engines filled the air, signaling the arrival of other people.

"So you losers finally decided to show up," Jason said as he finished unfolding the last of their chairs.

Nathan snorted as he hopped off his ATV. "Yeah, we would have been here sooner if Kate here got up earlier."

The young woman behind him pushed her visor up her face, revealing expressive green eyes. "Who the fuck gets up this early on a Saturday?" she groused as she swung her legs over the ATV.

"Hey, Kate," Matthew greeted Nathan's younger sister.

"Hey, Matt!" Kate hopped over to him and gave him a hug. "Congrats, man. On surviving your first week."

"Thanks." Beside him, Catherine stiffened, and her nostrils flared. Wait … was she jealous? That was ridiculous. Kate was like a sister to him. He tugged Catherine toward him and put a reassuring arm around her, ignoring the way her body tensed. "This is Catherine."

"Oh, you're Catherine," Kate said with a twinkle in her eye.

"You know who I am?" Catherine asked.

"Sybil warned me," she said. When Matthew cleared his throat, she added, "I mean she told me you were joining us today."

"Oh, that's nice of her," Catherine said in a chilly tone. "I—"

Kate threw her arms around Catherine. "It's nice to have new people over," she said as she squeezed tight. Catherine had a flabbergasted look on her face, but she returned the other woman's hug.

When Kate let go, she gave Matthew a wink. "She gives good hugs. I like her already."

Matthew grinned. Kate could be a bit much, especially to those who didn't know her, but Catherine seemed to relax.

"Kate, stop dicking around and help me!" Nate called as he began unloading their things.

"Keep your panties on, moron," she called. "I'm getting to know Matthew's ma—friend!"

Nathan flashed his sister the bird, then turned to Catherine and Matthew. "Hey Catherine!" he said with a grin and a wink.

"Hi, Nate," she said wryly.

Matthew put a possessive arm around Catherine. He knew he was being irrational, as Nathan would never try anything now that they all knew Catherine was his mate, but still, it was an instinctive gesture.

Two more ATVs arrived, and Matthew knew that had to be Ben and Luke. The two of them didn't live far from each other, and since Ben's cabin was much bigger, Luke had stored many of his things there, including his ATV.

"Are we late?" Ben asked as he approached them, all his things slung over one shoulder.

"Naw, we just got here. Catherine," he began, "this is my cousin, Benjamin Walker."

"Call me Ben," he said, extending his hand. Catherine took it, her hand dwarfed by his massive palm.

"Catherine," she said.

"Nice to meet ya, finally. I've seen you at The Den a couple of times, though," Ben said.

"Hello, Luke," Catherine greeted his adopted brother as he approached.

Dressed in nothing but his red flannel shirt, well-worn jeans, and snow clinging to his beard, Luke looked like a grizzled mountain man on steroids. He had a camping chair under one arm and a case of beer over his other shoulder. He gave her a grunt of acknowledgment and continued to walk to the spot where they were setting up the chairs.

"I can't imagine him sledding," Catherine said, her lips curling up at the corners of her mouth.

"He doesn't," Ben said. "He just likes to watch us tumble in the snow while he drinks beer."

"I think I'll be doing a lot of tumbling today," Catherine said, a worried look on her face.

"What, you never been sledding before?" Ben asked.

She shook her head.

"City girl, huh?"

"Something like that."

"Don't worry, I'm sure Matthew will teach you right," Ben said with a wink. "Well, lemme go put my things down and we can get started."

"So, you've never been sledding?" Matthew asked when they were alone.

She shook her head. "Nope." She didn't offer any other explanation, and he didn't press her. He would know everything about her in time, but for now, he supposed it was enough that she was by his side. He could sense there was still something bothering her, something dark behind her eyes. She was probably worried about the investigation, but Matthew was confident they could put it behind them soon. He had caught her glancing at her phone a couple of times that morning, but she said she was texting with her grandmother's neighbor, who she called when she realized she was stuck in Blackstone and needed someone to look after her.

"C'mon losers!" Kate shouted as she ran up the hill. "Last one down's a rotten egg!"

They spent the next two hours trudging up the hill and

then careening down at full speed on their sleds. Though she'd been wary at first, Catherine was laughing and screaming her lungs out as loud as the rest of them each time she slid down the slippery snow.

Tired, thirsty, and hungry, they all trudged back to their makeshift picnic site. Luke had started a fire and was already halfway through his case of beer. They all sat in their chairs and began to pass around the food and drinks.

"So, let me get this straight," Catherine said as she took a sip of her spiked hot cocoa. "You're dragons," she said as she pointed to Matthew, Jason, and Sybil. "And you're a bear," she gestured to Ben. "But you're cousins?"

Ben barked out a laugh. "Uh-huh."

"How does that even work?" she asked.

"Here's how," Jason began. "A long time ago, a dragon fucked a bear—"

"Oh, shut up," Ben said. "Let me tell it. I do it better." He cleared his throat. "A couple generations back, a Lennox dragon fell in love with a Walker bear. They mated, which created my side of the clan because dragons can't produce baby dragons with other shifters," he explained. "We branched off from the rest of the Walker clan and stuck around with the Lennoxes. You know how these dragons," he said jerking a thumb at Jason and Matthew, "are always getting into trouble."

"Ha!" Jason laughed. "I can burn down entire towns in five seconds."

Ben nodded. "Exactly. Bears are loyal and smart, dontcha know? We protect our own. Even from themselves."

"So, you're not *really* cousins anymore?" Catherine said.

"No, though we still like to call each other cousins."

"Wrong," Jason interjected. "*You* like to call us cousins. We can't get rid of you."

"Aww, no need to talk like that." Ben reached over to Jason, grabbed him by the neck and pulled him into a bear hug.

"What the fuck, man?" Jason choked as he spilled his drink and his body went sprawling on the snow-covered dirt.

"Shhh … it's okay, c'mere …" He rubbed his meaty hand over Jason's head. "I know you guys love me."

Nathan fell over laughing as Jason struggled to get away from Ben's bear hugs. Catherine herself looked like she couldn't stop herself from giggling. Her cheeks were pink from the exercise and the alcohol, and her braid had come undone some time ago. Matthew reached over and pushed a tendril away, and she looked up at him with her clear blue eyes, the blush on her face getting even redder.

They never did go back to sledding, but, instead, stayed gathered around the cozy fire, joking and laughing. Matthew let out a breath, the puff of air condensing in front of his face. When was the last time they were all gathered like this? Before he left for college? It was just like old times; the only one missing was Amelia, Ben's younger sister who was the same age as Sybil. She lived a few towns away, though she came back to Blackstone every now and then.

Glancing over at Catherine, he was glad to see that she was relaxed, laughing at the antics of his family and friends. Once in a while, he would catch her staring at him when she thought he wasn't looking. The thought made hope bloom inside him. His dragon was getting impatient. It wanted the mating bond, to tie her to him.

Matthew still wasn't quite sure what that bond was. He remembered that when his father had sat them down for "the talk" (among other things), all he said was, "You'll know it when it happens." Now he wished he wasn't a brooding pre-teen back then who was anxious to just get on with his life.

Had he known, he would have asked his father more questions.

"How about you, Catherine?" Sybil asked. "Any childhood antics to share? Embarrassing stories so the rest of us can feel good about ourselves?"

"Yeah!" Kate added. "Tell us! Were you a troublemaker like me or a good girl like Sybil?"

Catherine froze, her expression like the proverbial deer trapped in headlights. Matthew saw the fear in her eyes and cursed to himself. She was clamming up even more, and he wished he had thought to warn them not to bring up her past.

"I should get going," Luke said as he stood up, crushed his last empty can of beer in his hands, and tossed it into the now-full garbage bag he had brought along.

"Aww, Luke," Sybil whined. "You can't go. Meg is making us dinner back at the castle. I bet she has extra servings of her bread pudding for you."

"Sorry, Sybbie," he said, patting her head affectionately as he drew her in for a hug. "I got stuff to do. Later." He waved to the rest of us, then strode over to his ATV.

"Stuff to do, sure," Jason huffed as he watched Luke drive away. "Anyway, more pot roast for us. I do miss Meg's cooking. I'm getting tired of eating fast food all the time."

"Maybe you should find a girlfriend or a wife to cook for you," Sybil said. "Or a mate."

"Ugh, *no*," Jason said with a wave of his hand. "Look, that mating shit might be good for you all, but not for me. There's too much puss— er, variety in the world."

"Amen, brother," Nate agreed, raising a fist in the air and taking a sip of his beer.

"Really?" Sybil said. "Aren't you tired of chasing tail? The same shit, different girl?"

"You're such a romantic, Sybil. Why would I be tired?" Jason asked. "Don't you know it's the chase that makes it all worthwhile?"

"I thought it was busting a nut in some chick," Kate said dryly.

"That too," Jason laughed. "See, Nathan agrees."

"You all are such hypocrites," Kate said. "You change girls more often than you change underwear—don't look at me like that, Nate. We lived in the same house during your teenage years—yet when some guy tries to mess with me, Sybil, or Amelia, you all go scaring them off."

"Yeah, thanks to you, we're all going to die virgins," Sybil said.

"Speak for yourself," Kate added with a raised brow.

"Who the fuck is messing with you?" Nathan said as he shot to his feet.

"See? My point exactly." Kate said, crossing her arms over her chest.

"How about you, Ben?" Sybil asked. "Don't you want a mate?"

"Me?" Ben asked. "Sure. I just …"

"I'm sure Matthew agrees with me." She winked at Matthew.

"Well," Matthew said as he cleared his throat and got to his feet. "Meg will be waiting for us. You know she hates it when we're late." He glanced down at Catherine, who had a more relaxed look on her face. "Are you ready, sweetheart?"

She nodded and took the hand he offered. "Yeah, I'm getting cold."

He pulled her into his arms, letting his body heat warm her. Sybil cast him a knowing glance, while Jason gave him a thumbs-up sign. "Let's go home."

CHAPTER 12

DINNER WAS JUST AS LIVELY as their sledding picnic. As soon as they got into the castle and freshened up, dinner was waiting for them in the small dining room in the East Wing. Meg had prepared a feast for twenty people, which was just enough food for six shifters and one human.

Despite her smiles and laughter, there was a pang in Catherine's heart that wouldn't go away. How she missed this. Family. Bonding. Easy camaraderie. For a brief moment, she allowed herself to think of the distant past. Had it been so distant? Was she wrong in leaving behind what she had? But then, if she hadn't left, she wouldn't be here right now. She glanced over at Matthew, then turned away quickly.

No. These weren't good thoughts. She was getting too attached already. She just wanted one night to lose herself in Matthew's arms, and now here she was, having a family dinner with him. Mustering up all her determination, she solidified her resolve to leave. Maybe by tomorrow her contact will have replied. But she still needed to figure out a plan to get out of here. Blackstone was like a fortress, but she could find a way to escape. She'd done it before and under more difficult circumstances. When they had parked the ATVs in the garage, she saw more vehicles in there, as well as where they kept the keys. It wouldn't be difficult to leave in the middle of the night. She could tell Matthew she had a headache and wanted to sleep in the guest room tonight.

"We should get going," Jason said. "It's getting late."

"Yeah," Sybil agreed, glancing at her watch. "I had tons of fun though. I don't know why we don't do this anymore."

"It's 'cuz you're all busy adulting now," Kate said with a laugh.

They all stood up from the table, carrying their various dishes to the other room, which turned out to be a small kitchen. Meg and Christopher had gone home hours ago, so they didn't want to leave such a mess for them and the other staff to clean up tomorrow.

As soon as the dining room was clear and the dishwasher was filled, they all walked to the door said their goodbyes.

"It was nice meeting you, Catherine," Sybil said as they hugged.

"Maybe we'll be seeing more of you?" Kate asked. "It's nice not have such a sausage party around here all the time."

Catherine gave a nervous laugh. "I know, right?"

"Stay safe," Ben said as he pulled her into a tight hug. Now she knew why it was called bear hugs, as the gigantic man enveloped her with his body. "And don't let this grumpy dragon boss you around so much."

"I'll try," she said.

Jason and Nate said their goodbyes (with polite hand-shakes and a wary glance at Matthew for some reason), and soon everyone left the castle. She and Matthew were alone again.

"Did you have fun?" Matthew said as he came up behind her and placed a hand on her lower back.

"I did, actually." She was surprised herself. For the afternoon at least, she had forgotten her worries. She liked all of them, even foul-mouthed Kate. Catherine realized she'd been silly to feel jealous of her. Jealous? She shook her head mentally.

Yes, it was all going well, at least until the girls started asking about her past. It was a good thing Luke had saved her from having to lie to them, though she wondered if it was just good timing or deliberate.

"Are you okay?" Matthew asked as he led her up the stairs.

"Yeah ... I was just wondering ... if you don't mind my asking ... about Luke."

"Ah," he said. "Yeah, I'm sorry if he came off as rude and gruff. Well, the thing is he *is* rude and gruff."

"That's nothing to be sorry about," she replied. "But, I don't know, he seems lonely." And secretive.

"He doesn't like people. Except for us, maybe."

"How did your parents come to adopt him?"

"It's a long story," Matthew said.

"Oh, I didn't mean to pry."

"It's fine. It's not a secret or anything." He paused for a second as they stopped at the top of the staircase, then he led her to the East Wing. "Jason, Ben, Nathan, and I found him when we were kids."

"*Found* him?"

He nodded, his jaw tensing. "We were playing out back, and then we heard this strange noise. A lion cub came limping out of the bushes and collapsed right in front of us. It was covered in blood and scratches."

Catherine let out an involuntary gasp and then touched his

warm cheek with her palm. His eyes seemed far away, a hard glint behind the silvery depths. "What happened?"

"We called Mom and Dad, and they took him inside. They called a doctor who patched him up." His hand covered hers, and he turned his head to press a kiss to her wrists. Then, he tucked his hand under her arm and they began to walk. "Mom and Dad did everything they could to try and find his parents or any family. They called every lion pride they knew, even hired a PI to find his relatives. A whole year of looking and nothing. That's when they decided to adopt him legally."

"That was very generous of them," she said.

He shrugged. "What else could they have done? Luke had been living with us; no one else would take him in. They tried to find a pride who would adopt him, but even the nearest one wouldn't take him in. They have this thing about blood relation and didn't want anyone who wasn't born to them."

The thought hit a nerve. Who would be so mean? Lions, of course. They were proud creatures, among other things. "Well, sounds to me like Luke was better off being raised by your mom and dad."

"Yeah, well, you'd think so. Despite that rough exterior, he's a good person deep inside. Mom and Dad did their best. Mom especially." For a moment, there was a flash of hurt on his face.

"What's the matter? Did something else happen?"

He stopped and hesitated. "A story for another day. I don't really want to talk about Luke. Or anyone else." He nodded toward the door.

That cocky bastard. They were standing right in front of his room.

He opened the door and tugged her inside. As he closed the door behind him, he let out a deep sigh. "I love my family, but I've been waiting all day to get you alone," he whispered as he stepped closer.

"Matthew ..." Oh god, how she wanted this. Wanted him so bad she could feel it in her bones. It made her want to scream. "Then let's not talk anymore."

His kiss was rough, urgent, and sent whorls of heat straight to her core. Sliding his hands down her thighs, he lifted her up and wrapped her legs around his waist, letting her feel his erection through his trousers.

Matthew walked them to the bed and then lowered her on it. He stood back and began to remove the layers of clothes on his body. She did the same, peeling the snow pants down her legs and the sweater over her head. When he was fully naked, he climbed on the bed and removed the rest of her clothing.

"I want you so bad," he said as he crawled over her and covered her with his body.

"Me, too," she replied and wrapped her arms around his neck to bring him down for a kiss.

He took her mouth with such savage intensity, it scared her. But something inside her was saying she shouldn't be afraid of him. She was still planning on leaving, but well, one last time wouldn't hurt.

His hand slid down her belly and cupped her mound. She was already wet and ready for him. He moaned against her mouth as a finger entered her warmth. She lifted her hips, eager for more. Her body exploded in a quick, intense orgasm.

He shifted away, reaching for the condoms in his nightstand. She closed her eyes and sighed, then felt his fingers touch her slick lips. She let out a whimper when he moved his fingers away, but her disappointment was short-lived when she felt the head of his thick cock pushing into her.

"Catherine," he whispered as he stared down at her.

Her eyes fluttered open, and her heart thudded in her chest when she looked up. The expression on his face was intense, and his eyes seemed to burn with a fire she'd never seen before. Whatever it was, it was like she was feeling it too and it wanted to burn her alive. It scared her. And thrilled her.

She swallowed the lump forming in her throat. "Matthew ... I ..." The words evaporated in the air as he began to move. Rough, wild, passionate. He didn't start slow or deliberate, and she didn't care. The pressure building in her was threatening to burst. Matthew pulled her ankles over his shoulders, and the sensation was too much as he drove into her. She couldn't remember what she said or did. Maybe she cried out his name or raked her nails down his arms till she left marks. All she could remember was the pure, white heat that exploded from her body as her orgasm ripped through her.

He cried out her name as he thrust into her one last time. With a groan, he fell on top of her, bracing himself on his forearms, so his full weight wasn't on her. He lay his head between her breasts and closed his eyes.

Seconds ticked by. Catherine's head was muddled. *What happened?*

Matthew pushed himself up and stared down at her. He brushed her hair away from her face. "Catherine ... I think ... you're mine. You're my mate."

She was stunned into silence.

"I know this sounds crazy," he continued. "You probably don't understand because you're human."

She gasped. And her heart broke into a million pieces because she understood better than he thought. *More lies upon lies.*

"Do you want to talk about it?"

"I … I'm tired." It was true.

He nodded and kissed her forehead. "We can talk tomorrow." He rolled off her and climbed out of the bed.

She turned to her side, away from him, and closed her eyes. When the door to the bathroom closed, she let out a breath she didn't realize she'd been holding. *Mates?*

"Oh no."

It couldn't be. He was wrong. This whole thing was wrong. She didn't want a mate.

"Catherine?"

She whipped around. Even as her brain told her to run and flee, her treacherous little heart made her stay put. Oh no, indeed.

"Are you alright?" he asked as he climbed back into bed.

She pasted a smile on her face. "Yeah, I am. As I said, I'm just tired."

He pulled the sheets back and climbed underneath. "Then we'll get some rest. We can talk in the morning."

Her body was aching, and her lids felt heavy. She was tired, so she slipped under the sheets, and he pulled her to him.

Morning would come too soon.

CHAPTER 13

CATHERINE'S SLEEP was deep and dreamless. It was probably from yesterday's activities. But the moment she did awaken, she was up with a start.

Matthew.

He was still asleep, thankfully. God, he looked handsome, even in his sleep. He was lying on his stomach, his face turned to her. A lock of hair fell over his forehead, and she ached to brush it aside.

No, she had to get out of there.

All this crazy talk about mates. A pain pricked at her, something she hadn't felt in years. And more memories flooded her mind, ones she'd thought were long since buried, only making themselves known in her dreams.

No. She was no one's mate. Not now, not ever.

Carefully, she crept out of bed. It would take her too long to get dressed in the clothes she had worn yesterday, so she grabbed his shirt and slipped it on. Big mistake as now she could smell *him*. But she couldn't waste any more time, not if she wanted to get away.

She crept out and made her way back to her room. It was a good thing she didn't even unpack. Grabbing the cleanest clothes she had, she quickly dressed. She put her coat and boots on, then slung her bag over her shoulder as she raced for the door.

"Catherine?"

Matthew's bewildered face greeted her as she yanked the door open. "M-M-Matthew. You're up."

"I'm up?" he asked in an incredulous voice. "What are you —" he stopped short as his gaze landed on her bag. "Are you leaving?"

What could she say? She was hoping for a quick exit, but it was too late.

"Was it because of what I said last night?" He ran his hands through his hair.

"No, I—"

"Then tell me!" His eyes turned stormy, and his hands gripped her arms. "Why are you running away?"

"I'm not," she said in a flat tone. "And please let go of me."

"You're not getting away from me," he said with a growl. "I told you, we're mates. You're going to stay here."

His words rang in her head. "You can't keep me here against my will!" she shouted as she wrenched away from him. "I—"

"Matthew!"

They both stopped and turned to the source of the voice. Meg was sprinting down the hallway. She stopped in front of them, her breath coming in deep gasps. "Matthew ... you have ... to come ... quick ..."

"What's wrong, Meg?"

"Chief Meacham," she said when she caught her breath. "He's here. And he's not alone."

Matthew's face became a stone-cold mask. "Stay here," he said, his voice deadly serious. "Are they out front?"

Meg nodded.

"Let's go."

Catherine watched him walk away, her heart thudding in her chest. Dread filled her gut. It was a Sunday morning, so she knew it wasn't good news. There was no running now.

Ignoring Matthew's order, she hurried down the hall and took the grand staircase two steps at a time. The front door was half open with Meg standing next to it. When the house-keeper tried to stop Catherine, she brushed the older woman away.

"Chief Meacham," she greeted. She saw Matthew tense visibly when she appeared, but he said nothing.

Meacham was wearing his full uniform, hat on his head, and aviator sunglasses that obscured his eyes. "Miss Archer," he said. "Glad to see you're up. Mr. Lennox said you were indisposed."

"What do you want?"

"You're going to have to come with me."

"What for?" she asked.

"I'm afraid you're under arrest." He waved a white envelope in front of her.

"No!" she cried. "I didn't do it! I swear! I've never even owned a gun or fired one! I didn't kill Jack Cunningham."

Meacham's mouth pulled into a grim line. "I'm not here to arrest you for his murder."

"You're not?" Now she was confused.

He shook his head. "No. We're arresting you and extra-diting you back to California to answer charges for the murder of Clarissa Benton and Ivan Chesnovak."

"What?" The edges of her vision blurred, and her knees

buckled. She braced herself against the door. "I didn't kill them. Please, you have to believe me."

"I've seen the evidence myself," Meacham said. "Your prints are all over the place and the murder weapon was found in your things. D.A. says it was a love triangle gone wrong."

"That's preposterous. I didn't do it!" She looked at Matthew. His face was inscrutable, his jaw hard and his eyes looking straight at Meacham.

"I have to do my job, Miss Archer," Meacham said. "Now, please turn around and put your hands behind you—"

"No."

Matthew's words were like a knife, cutting through the air around them.

Meacham took his sunglasses off. "Excuse me?" His eyes had that unearthly glow. *Of course, he was a shifter, too,* Catherine thought.

"You will not lay a hand on her," Matthew said, his voice deadly serious. "If you want her, you will go through me."

Meacham put his sunglasses into his front shirt pocket and shook his head. Then, he raised a hand in the air. A dozen red laser dots appeared on Matthew's chest. "I don't want to do this, Matthew," he said. "You know when I lost that last election for sheriff, it was your father who helped me become Police Chief here. But I swore to carry out the law and that's what I have to do. I've brought back up. I've got snipers ready to pump you full of sedatives. They've been told to fire if they see even one scale or claw."

"Don't!" Catherine cried. "Please …" She looked at Matthew, then back at Meacham. "I'll go. You don't have to cuff me."

"I—"

"You can cuff me in the car." She didn't want Matthew upset. Didn't want to see him shot down. "Let's go."

Meacham nodded and took her arm, then led her to the waiting police car. She didn't even glance behind her as they drove away.

Matthew stood still, his body numb, as he watched Meacham take Catherine away. Inside him, his dragon was screaming and roaring to get out.

He had hesitated. His mate was faced with wild accusations, and he had waited to defend her. Stood there and did nothing. Because he was hurt. Hurt that she had snuck away from his bed and that he had caught her about to run away. Why, he asked himself. He had told her she was his mate; he was ready to give her the world if she wanted it. But she threw it in his face like it was nothing. His heart was breaking, and he wanted to hurt her, too.

But his dragon wouldn't let him. *Mine.* It knew that Catherine was in trouble. It didn't care about the law or justice. No, their mate couldn't be guilty. She wasn't a murderer. She was good and kind. It was clawing its way out of him, ready to fight anyone who would dare take her away.

Now he wished he had his dragon's resolve. His own stubborn, analytical mind was telling him that it made sense. It explained why she was so secretive and why she was running away. *She was guilty.* Meanwhile, his broken, hurt heart was doing nothing to defend her.

Yet still, she protected him, didn't want to see him hurt. Like a good mate would do.

"Matthew!" Meg cried. "What are you doing?"

"Huh?"

"For God's sake! She's your mate, right? Why did you just let her go?"

"What was I supposed to do, Meg?" he asked. "I was ready to fight for her. My dragon was ready to burn anyone who would take her away, but those tranquilizers would have taken me down anyway." *Coward!* his dragon seemed to roar.

"You don't think it's true? That she murdered two people?"

"No, of course not."

"Then go after her," she said. She put up her hand when he opened his mouth. "No, I'm not talking about turning into a dragon and burning up the entire police department. Go be *with* her. Tell her you believe her and that you're going to stick by her side no matter what."

"Damn." Meg was right. "Call Sorkin," he said. "Haul him out of bed; I don't care. Tell him to be at the police station when I get there, or I'm going to find another lawyer for Lennox Corp."

Meg held out her hand. His keys were in her palm. "Go."

Matthew gave Meg a grateful smile and grabbed his keys. He was going after her. It wasn't too late. He jumped into his Range Rover and revved up the engine, before tearing down the dirt roads. They hadn't been gone too long, so he could probably catch up with them. No, wait. He'd keep a respectable distance, in case they thought he'd changed his mind and was going to try and bust her free. He would do this the right way. He would pay whatever bail they asked and make sure she never saw the inside of a cell. Because he was positive she couldn't be guilty.

He knew these roads like the back of his hand, so he drove slowly. Hopefully, Sorkin would already be on the way. In a couple of hours, he would have arranged her release. Or he would fly out to L.A. and hire the best attorney there. It didn't matter. This was something he was going to face with her, and when they put it behind them, it would be only a distant memory.

The sound of the explosion in the distance shook him out of his fantasy. He didn't know how, but he was sure Catherine was in danger. He slammed his foot on the gas. This time, he would not hesitate.

CHAPTER 14

CATHERINE SLUMPED BACK in the seat of the patrol car and stared up at the ceiling. She had just been arrested and was possibly going to prison for the rest of her life for a crime she didn't commit. Yet, all she could think of was the look on Matthew's face when she stood there, being accused of murder. He couldn't even look at her. Did he believe them?

Of course he did. He caught her about to run away again. Only guilty people ran away. In a way, maybe she was guilty. If she had stayed and gone to the police, she would have helped put away those bastards who killed Rissa. But she was so damn scared. The Chesnovak Brotherhood was too notorious. There would have been a trial, and her face would have been all over the news. And then the truth of who she *really* was would come out.

"What the fuck is going on?" Meacham cursed, and the car screeched to a halt. Catherine let out a cry and braced herself against the glass between the front and back seat.

"Who the hell is that?" Meacham's deputy said.

Silence. Then chaos.

There was an explosion, and a split second later, the world turned upside down. Her body was whipped around like a rag doll, and her brain scrambled in her skull. When she opened her eyes, her vision was blurry, but based on the position of her body, she knew she was lying down on the roof of the car. Slowly, she struggled to get upright.

"Chief!" she cried, as she banged on the bullet proof glass.

Meacham let out a moan and reached for his seatbelt. "Stay … in here …" he said as he struggled with the buckle.

The door of the car was suddenly thrown open. No, it was torn away, the sound of metal ripping apart unmistakable. She screamed when a hand reached inside, grabbed her, pulled her out, then dropped her to the ground.

"There you are," a voice said. "We finally have you."

She froze, recognizing the tone and accent. Slowly, her vision came into focus and she recognized the man. Tall and imposing, with cruel, light blue eyes. His blond hair was cropped close to his head, and tattoos crawled out under the neck of his shirt and down his arms. This was the man who had killed Rissa. *Andrei*. Behind him, several men stood, carrying various weapons. It seemed he didn't come alone.

Andrei tsked. "Did you think you could get away from us?" he asked. "Did you think you could run from The Brotherhood?" He let out a cruel laugh. "You slipped away from us once, but I'm here to finish the job."

Fuck. She had to distract him. Or delay him. Surely someone would have heard that explosion. They probably used a rocket launcher of some sort. She'd overheard Ivan bragging about those kinds of weapons before. "How did you find me?"

"That slimy hyena, of course. Best tracker in the business. Unfortunately, he's also a very dead tracker."

"You killed him? But why?"

"Because that two-faced sonofabitch wanted more money before he gave us your location," he sneered. "He said he found someone else who would pay more for the information and that if we didn't double his fee, he would turn you over to them instead. But that fool didn't know we were also tracking him. We didn't need his information anymore." He grabbed her collar and hauled her to her feet. "So, where is it? Tell me now, and I'll make sure your death is painless."

"What?" she cried. "What are you talking about?"

"The money!" Andrei shoved her down on the ground and forced her to her knees. Something cold and hard pressed against her temples and a cocking sound rang in her ear.

"W-w-what money? What are you talking about?"

"The money my stupid cousin Ivan and his little whore stole! Why did you think I killed them?"

"I don't know anything about any money!" Oh god. This was it. She was going to die now. The only thing she could think of was Matthew. Her heart sank. She had been so afraid of what would happen if they did become mates and he died and left her that she didn't even think of what would happen to him if she were gone. But she already knew the answer. She had seen it unfold as she grew up.

"Stupid girl!" He slapped her with the side of the gun so hard she fell over. The pain was unbearable; the entire side of her face was on fire. "That little whore didn't have anyone else. No family, no friends. Only you. Who else would she have trusted with half a million dollars?"

"Half a million …" *Oh, Rissa. Why?* "I swear, she didn't tell me about the money."

"Stop lying and tell me!" He pointed the gun at her again.

"I don't know! I swear!"

The sound of tires screeching on pavement made them both start. Andrei whipped his head around, then let out a string of angry curses in Russian. The men around him began to move.

Catherine looked up. She saw a figure leap out of the car. *Matthew!* Her heart pounded against her chest, and she could barely breathe.

The air around them grew cold, and everyone stopped. Then, Matthew began to change.

"No!" Andrei cried. "Get him!" More guns cocked and then there was the sound of rapid gunshots.

But it was too late. Matthew's dragon ripped out of him so fast, his human form was barely a blur. A fifty-foot dragon with golden scales and razor-sharp claws stood before them, spreading its wings and tossing its head back with a roar. The cold air turned hot as fire began to spew from its mouth.

Catherine watched in awe at the sight of Matthew's dragon raining down flames. She barely heard the popping sound, and only realized she'd been shot when she felt the pain in her side.

"You idiot!" Andrei screamed. "We need her alive! She hasn't told us the location of the money."

"I'm sorry!" someone cried. "But we need to get out of here! Look at that thing!"

"Coward!"

Catherine slumped down to the ground. God, it was so painful. Then, she felt her body begin to grow cold. She looked up, watching the dragon as it continued to bring hell on earth while she lay there bleeding.

The dragon let out a roar, a stream of fire shooting from its mouth, targeting the lions surrounding him. It wasn't much of a contest. There were only about a dozen of them. When they started firing and realized ordinary bullets only bounced off his scales, they threw their guns down and began to shift.

Lions!

They surrounded him, and the fastest one managed to climb on his back but was tossed away with one flick of a claw. Years of practice and working in the mines had helped Matthew perfect his aim, and he could carefully direct the flame so as not to hurt anyone in the vicinity. Though today, he was doing the opposite.

The smell of charred flesh filled the air, and he let out a puff of smoke. Where was his mate? He swung his gigantic body around and saw three men standing over a small figure on the ground. The dragon let out a roar and swung its gigantic body around.

"Run!" one of them said.

His dragon roared for revenge, but the sight of Catherine on the ground made Matthew stop. He quickly pushed the dragon deep down inside of him and changed back. *Please let her be okay.* But as the smell of blood hit his nose, he knew she wasn't.

"No!" he cried as he knelt down in front of her. Catherine was lying on the ground, her hand clutched to her side. "Catherine … don't move …. no, don't try to talk! Stay with me, sweetheart. Please." *Think.* His car was still intact, but it would take too long to drive her. She was losing too much blood. She'd be too weak to hold onto him if he flew, though. So, he picked her up gently, then carried her to his car. Carefully, he put her in the back seat.

"Hang on, Catherine. Please."

He slammed the door shut, then quickly began to change into his dragon form. Once he was fully transformed, he dug his talons into the car. With a flap of his wings, he was airborne. Matthew pushed his dragon faster and harder than he'd ever done in his whole life. He soared over Blackstone until, finally, he landed in front of the Lucas Lennox Memorial Hospital. As he set down the vehicle, the dragon let out a loud roar, hoping it would get the staff's attention.

The dragon hopped back as medical personnel began to stream out of the hospital's door. Matthew quickly changed back to his human form and grabbed the nearest nurse he could.

"Gunshot wound victim in the back of the car," he barked at her.

"We'll take care of it, Mr. Lennox," she said with a nod. "We need a stretcher!" she called to the rest of the staff. "And get an OR ready NOW."

Behind him, two ambulances roared to life and sped out the driveway. "Where are they going?" he asked a passing nurse.

"To Castle Road, Mr. Lennox," she answered. "Got a dispatch. From the Sheriff's office."

"Fuck!" The police car and the escorts had been overturned when he arrived, but Meacham was alive. Probably not in very good condition. Plus, there were still three lions out there.

He ran across the pavement, then pushed his dragon out, its claws barely touching the ground as he flew away. He went back toward the castle, using his enhanced vision to scan below for any sign of the lions.

There!

The three of them had gathered in a clearing. *Idiots.* They were dressed in fancy leather shoes and jackets. Probably from the city. And, obviously, they'd never encountered a dragon before. As he drew closer, three heads looked up. More curses in Russian, then they scattered. Not that it did them any good. The dragon flapped its mighty wings and chased after two of them, raining down a stream of fire until they were nothing but ashes.

He landed in front of the third man, then grabbed him with his claws.

The dragon began to shrink, scales turning into skin, claws turning to hands. "Who are you? And who sent you?" Matthew roared, squeezing the man's neck.

"Che-Chesnovak Brotherhood Pride," he choked out.

Matthew threw him to the ground. "What do you want with my mate?"

"She ... she knows where the money is!" he cried. "The Alpha wanted his money back. Please don't kill me!"

"I'm not going to kill you," he said. "I want you to go back to your Alpha and tell him that she is mate to the Blackstone Dragon, and I will turn every single one of you into ash if he tries to harm her again!"

"I-I-I will tell him!"

"Now go!"

The man scrambled to his feet, then sprinted toward the woods like a bat out of hell. *Good riddance.*

Matthew turned back into his dragon form once again and took to the skies. Sweeping back toward the site of the attack, he saw a couple of people in uniform walking about, helping others climb out from their cars. The sound of sirens was drawing closer, so he assumed help was near. He went in the opposite direction, back to the hospital.

CHAPTER 15

As soon as he stormed through the doors of the hospital, someone handed him an extra set of clothes, which he took gratefully. He went to the bathroom, cleaned up as best he could, and put on the clothes. When he exited, James Lawton, the director of the hospital, was waiting for him.

"Where is she?" he asked.

"Right this way, Mr. Lennox," James fawned as he led him to the waiting room right outside the OR. "I'm personally taking care of everything. She's still on the table, and we have all our best staff working to make sure she's okay."

"Will she make it?"

James swallowed a gulp. "I'm afraid only the surgeon can answer that question. Can I get you a coffee? Tea? Anything at all."

"No."

He sat down on the uncomfortable bench and clasped his hands together, his eyes staring at the white wall.

"Mr. Lennox …"

"Go," he said in a cold voice. "I'd like to be alone. I only want to see the surgeon when they're done."

"Of course, Mr. Lennox," James said. "Please don't hesitate to call me for anything at all."

Matthew sat there, unmoving, for a long time. When he closed his eyes, all he could see was Catherine's limp body on the ground, blood pouring out of her side. So, he kept his eyes open.

"Matthew!"

He whipped his head around. Jason and Sybil were running down the hallway, Ben not far behind.

"Oh, Matthew!" Sybil cried as she sat down beside him. She wrapped an arm around him and drew him into a hug.

"What are you doing here?" he asked.

"I saw your dragon flying overhead," Ben said. "Then I called Jason to check if it was him or you. He called Meg, and she told us that Catherine had been arrested. Then we heard there was a commotion and came straight to town."

"What happened?" Jason asked, his expression serious.

Matthew took a deep breath and began to explain, at least the parts he understood.

"Lions? What the fuck is a pride of lions doing here in Blackstone? They weren't from Thunder Valley?" Jason said, mentioning the name of the nearest pride.

"No," Matthew said. "Said they were from The Chesnovak Brotherhood Pride. Looked like city people."

"What did they want with Catherine?" Ben asked, scratching his head. "Did it have anything to do with her arrest?"

"All he said was something about money."

"Shit. Maybe you shouldn't have torched all of them," Jason said. "We could get more answers."

"I don't give a shit about answers," Matthew growled. "All I want is for Catherine to be okay."

"She will be," Sybil reassured him. "You did the right thing, getting her back here as soon as you could."

Nate and Kate came soon after, and, much to his surprise, so did Luke. His brother had a grave look on his face, even more so than usual, but he didn't say anything. Instead, he sat beside Matthew and put a reassuring hand on his shoulder. He looked up at Luke and gave him a grateful nod.

The hours ticked by. No word from the OR. Sybil and Ben were trying to talk to the nurses, but they couldn't say anything more than what they already knew. She was still in the OR. No, they didn't have any updates.

Sheriff Meacham also dropped by. He looked busted up, but the cuts on his face were already healing. "I'm sorry, Matthew," he said as he sat down on the opposite bench. "I should have believed her." He told them of what he had heard of the conversation between Catherine and the leader of the group of lions. It didn't tell them anything he didn't already know, except to confirm Catherine was innocent of everything. "I've already contacted the LAPD. Their D.A. will be dropping all charges, and there will be no extradition."

That at least brought some relief to Matthew, but he knew that pain in his chest wouldn't go away until she was in the clear.

Finally, the OR doors opened. A doctor in surgical scrubs stepped out.

"Mr. Lennox? They told me you were the one who brought in Ms. Archer. I'm Dr. Parry."

"Is she going to be okay?"

Dr. Parry's face never faltered. "I'm afraid it's still too early to tell. Good news is the bullet went through. However, it did graze her liver, though only the outer capsule. Still, she lost a lot of blood. You brought her in just in time."

"Can we see her?" Sybil asked.

"I'm afraid not."

Matthew stepped forward. "I need to see her."

"There's nothing to see, Mr. Lennox," Dr. Parry said in a serious voice. "She just got out of surgery and can't be disturbed. Medical personnel only."

Mathew opened his mouth to protest, but Jason put a hand on his shoulder. "Maybe we should just let her rest. She'll be better in the morning."

Matthew wanted to believe that. "Thank you, doctor."

The doctor excused himself, telling them he was going to check on Catherine again once she was settled in the ICU.

"You should probably get some sleep. You've had a long day," Jason said. "You can stay with me, I'm closer."

"No," Matthew said. "I'm staying here."

"You're a mess—"

"You need to rest—"

"You can't do anything—"

"STOP."

Five pairs of eyes turned to Luke. He stood up, his arms crossed over his massive chest. "He should stay if he wants to," Luke gruffed. "I'll be here."

"You don't have to stay," Matthew said.

"You know I don't sleep anyway," Luke retorted. "If you don't want these guys to force you to go home, then you'll let me stay with you."

"Fine," Matthew relented.

Luke nodded. "Good. You all should go home." He turned to Jason. "Matthew won't be going to work tomorrow. You know what will happen if the CEO of Lennox doesn't show up at the office."

"Panic," Jason said. "'Matthew Lennox will be there, bright and early."

"Sybbie," Luke said. "Try to see if you can contact Hank and Riva. They should know what's happening."

"Already on it."

Luke nodded to Nate and Ben. "The mines. You guys are in charge. Keep things going and everyone calm."

"Of course," Ben agreed, and Nate nodded.

"I'll come back in the morning with some fresh clothes for you," Kate volunteered. She wrinkled her nose at Matthew. "And deodorant. Don't want Catherine smelling you after what you've been through today."

Matthew smiled. "Thank you, Kate."

They all said their goodbyes, and, soon, Luke and Matthew were alone.

"Thank you, Luke," Matt said, as they sat down.

Luke took the bench opposite him. "It's gonna be a long night. If you want to close your eyes, go ahead. I'll wake you up if anything happens."

———

Matthew didn't think he was that tired, but as soon as his head hit the pillow one of the nurses had brought him, he fell into a deep sleep. He had never shifted between his human and dragon form so many times in one day, and it had taken its toll on his body. A couple of times, he heard the footsteps of passing nurses, but someone, Luke most likely, put a reassuring hand on his shoulder and he went back to sleep.

The smell of fresh coffee perked up his senses. He opened his eyes and quickly closed them again as the fluorescent light overhead nearly blinded him. Sitting up on the bench, he rubbed a palm down his face.

"You look like shit," Kate said as she plopped down next to him. Sybil sat on the other side and gave him a reassuring hug. "Here." She dumped a bag on his lap. It was warm and smelled like fried dough.

Surprisingly, he didn't feel like shit after a full night's sleep. His mind was clear. But he was definitely hungry. He reached into the bag, grabbed a donut, and ate it, and then another and another, until he finished the entire bag. Kate handed him another bag, though this one had fresh clothes and, as she had promised, deodorant. A nurse led him into an empty room, where he used the bathroom to take a quick shower and change.

When he got back from the bathroom after washing up, Kate, Luke, and Sybil were already on their feet, and Dr. Parry was there.

"Mr. Lennox," Dr. Parry said. "The nurses told me you stayed all night. There was no need for that."

"How is she?" he asked, urgency in his voice.

"She's stable. That's about all I can tell you."

"Isn't there anything else you can do?" he asked, his hands fisted at his sides.

"At this stage, it's a little too early to be discussing further treatments. She's not out of the woods quite yet, but we can talk about—"

"Excuse me, doctor," a voice from behind them said. "I don't think you should be discussing a patient's treatment with non-family members."

Matthew froze. The voice was familiar and, at the same time, *not*. The accent was posh and refined, the tone biting. He swung around, and his heart stopped.

Standing in front of them was a cool, blond beauty, dressed in a white wool coat, stiletto heels, and hair done in a sophisticated updo. As he focused on her face, blue eyes stared right back, piercing straight through him.

His eyes and brain were battling with his dragon. *Not our mate.* Matthew didn't know how long they all stared at her with stunned looks on their faces.

"C-C-Catherine?" Sybil managed to choke out.

She shook her head. "No, I'm Christina. Catherine is my twin sister." She turned to Dr. Parry. "I'm here to take her home."

"Home?" Matthew said, trying to control his anger.

Christina ignored him. "I'm her next of kin, so I'll be in charge of her care. Is there anywhere we can speak in private, doctor? Away from these *strangers*."

"I ... uh ..." Dr. Perry looked at Matthew with hesitation in his eyes.

"I could show you my passport," she added. "But that would only confirm what's obvious."

Dr. Parry shook his head. "I'm sure it's fine. We can, uh, go to one of the meeting rooms."

"Wait, you can't just leave us out of this!" Matthew growled. His dragon was furious and wanted to turn its anger on this ... impostor.

"Matthew saved her," Sybil pointed out.

Christina whipped around and pinned Matthew with her gaze. "I know who you are and that your name is all over this hospital," she sneered. "But, legally, you have no connection to her. So please just leave, and I'll take care of my sister. You've done *enough*."

Dr. Parry gave him an apologetic look. "Right this way, Ms. Archer."

"It's Stavros," she corrected and allowed Dr. Parry to lead her away.

"Holy shit," Kate said. "Catherine has a twin?"

"Apparently," Sybil said. "Did you know, Matthew? Of course not. So, who the heck is she, really?"

Matthew's jaw hardened. "I don't know. But it doesn't matter. Catherine is not leaving." At least, not until he had a chance to see her. "I have to talk Catherine somehow."

They went to James Lawton's office to see if he could do anything.

"I'm sorry, Mr. Lennox," he said in an apologetic voice. "You know I'd do anything I can for you, but this is a legal matter, and, as a family member, she does have rights. Perhaps you could consult your lawyer?"

Matthew got on the phone with Sorkin, but he didn't have any good news for them either. "Legally, we have no standing. If Ms. Archer's sister wants to take her to another medical facility for treatment, then she has every right to. We could argue that it would be better for her health to stay here, but I need a courtroom and a judge."

"Do what you can," Matthew said, trying not to sound desperate.

They ended up losing the whole morning running around, trying to find a way to get more information about Catherine's condition or ways to see her. But Christina must have gotten to the administration, as every nurse and doctor they tried to talk to immediately shut up, citing privacy laws. They didn't even know if she was conscious, though a kind nurse had reassured them she was alive and stable.

"Who the fuck is this woman?" Kate huffed, kicking a nearby garbage can.

"Maybe we can sneak into Catherine's room?" Sybil asked.

It took a lot of legwork (and bribery), but they found out her room number. When they reached it, there was a very large, imposing figure in a suit standing guard in front of the door. The man's face was drawn into an intimidating, cold scowl and anyone passing by the room avoided looking at him or even getting near him.

"*Wolf*," Luke growled.

Kate and Sybil stopped in their tracks and looked at Matthew.

"What the fuck is a wolf doing there, standing guard?" Kate asked.

It seemed like there were more layers that hid Catherine's true identity than Matthew thought. "I don't know."

"Wait." Sybil grabbed her phone and tapped on the screen. She showed them the grainy photo on her phone—an older, dark-haired man with an arrogant expression on his face. "Stavros. As in, *Aristotle Stavros*."

"What? The Greek billionaire?" Kate said. "And Alpha of the Lykos Pack?"

"Uh-huh." She scrolled further on the screen. "Hmmm … there's not much about him. But then he's known to be very secretive. A recluse. No one's seen or heard from him in years."

"Is Catherine a wolf shifter?" Sybil asked.

"No way," Kate said. "We all would have known. She can't hide *that*."

"I don't care," Matthew interjected. "I just want this over

with. We have to find a way into that room." Preferably one that didn't involve him turning that wolf bodyguard into ashes, but he wasn't picky at this point.

"Alrighty then," Kate said, cracking her knuckles. "Let's go find that biotch, and Luke, when she comes around the corner, you grab her—"

"We are not getting rid of her," Sybil said.

Kate snorted. "We're only going to keep her away until Matthew's convinced Catherine that they're mates and she agrees to marry him and pop out a dozen baby dragons."

"Why Kate, I never knew you were a romantic," Sybil said in a sarcastic tone.

"Pfffft." She picked at an imaginary piece of lint on her jacket. "I just don't want a grumpy dragon moping around that castle."

"Hold on. Kate's got the right idea." Matthew said. "We just have to distract her for a couple of hours and then get rid—I mean incapacitate—the wolf guard."

"I may have an idea," Sybil said. "We'll need some help, but I bet we could pull it off."

"A plan?" Kate said. "Like when we were kids, and we tried to steal the Verona Mills mascot?"

"Something like that," Sybil said with a twinkle in her eye. "Christina can't stay in the hospital forever. With Catherine's condition, she probably needs to stay for a while, plus they probably have some plan to transport her. We have to find out where Christina is staying and how she got here. Then, we keep her away, and take down the guard."

"With what?" Luke asked.

"This is a hospital," Kate said. "Don't worry, I know how to get into the storage room and get the right drugs to knock him out."

"Why would you know how to do that?" Matthew asked.

"Oh Matthew," she said, patting him on the shoulder. "You could only dream of the things I know how to do."

They'd been running around the hospital so much that Lawton offered his office as a sort of meeting point. Sybil called around, and it didn't take long to get more information about Christina. A private jet registered to Stavros Shipping landed at the Verona Mills airport this morning. There was also a "C. Stavros" staying at the Ritz Ski Resort about thirty miles out of town, near one of the more popular skiing slopes in the area.

"I just saw Christina leave," Kate said, as she rushed back into the room. She'd been following Christina around the hospital. "I bet she's on the way to her hotel, but we know she'll be back at some point. Now, I have several ideas on how we can keep her away."

A lightbulb lit up in Matthew's head. "I know how. Jason."

"Jason?"

He nodded. "He's already pretending to be me at the office," he said. "He can keep the charade going. He can stake out the Ritz, and if he sees her leaving, warn us and intercept her. Pretend that he wants to talk or something."

"Brilliant," Sybil said. "Call Jason and let him know the plan. Once we know she's secure, we'll figure out how to get into that room."

"This is a crazy plan," Luke said.

"No, it's brilliant," Kate said. "Come with me, Luke. You'll be my lookout while I raid the supply room for whatever drugs I can get my hands on. Worst case scenario, I'll dump an entire bottle of Ex-Lax into a cup of coffee and flirt with him a bit to get him to drink it." The two of them walked away, leaving Sybil and Matthew alone.

"This is going to work," Sybil assured him.

Matthew said nothing but nodded. He sure hoped so.

CHAPTER 16

CATHERINE FELT like she was swimming in a vat of molasses, going in and out of consciousness like her head was bobbing up and down in the dark, syrupy liquid. There were voices, lots of voices around her, but she couldn't make out what they were saying. Her body felt numb, but as she began to wake up, the pain started to creep in. *I was shot.*

Her mind began to piece things together. The Brotherhood attacking them. Andrei. And Matthew's dragon.

God, he was a scary beast. But he'd come for her. To rescue her. Where was she now?

The scratchy sheets under her fingers and the antiseptic smell gave it away. *The hospital.* How did she get here?

She tried to sit up, but a pain in her side forced her back down. It hurt terribly, but at least she was awake and alive. The low light in the room made it difficult to see what was around her, but the call button just above her head was like a beacon. Before she could reach for it, a growl and then a thud from outside made her stop.

Alarm bells in her head made her freeze. For a second, she

thought she was in danger. That the lions were still after her. However, when the door opened and a familiar figure walked in, she breathed a sigh of relief.

"Matthew," she rasped out, realizing her throat was dry and itchy. She braced her hand on the mattress, so she could prop herself up and reach for the glass of water she spied on the table beside the bed.

"Catherine? Are you awake? I—what are you doing?" Matthew sprinted toward her.

"Water."

Matthew grabbed the glass and held it to her lips. The liquid felt soothing as it went down her dry throat.

"Slow down," he said. "You might choke."

She finished half the glass before she allowed him to take it away. God, even swallowing was tiring, and she fell back on the bed. Matthew moved closer to her and placed his warm palm on her cheek. That felt good, too.

"I was so afraid I'd lost you," he whispered. "When I saw those men—"

"The Brotherhood," she said. "What happened?"

"I took care of them, sweetheart," he said, his voice going cold. "They'll never bother you again."

She breathed a sigh of relief. "I believe you," she said. "But I should probably explain. And tell you the truth."

"Shhhh …" he soothed. "The only thing that matters is that you're alive and you're going to be okay."

"Please, I need to tell you the truth," she said. "I don't want to go on lying to you. I can't."

Matthew brushed her hair aside and then laid a gentle kiss on her forehead. "Alright, sweetheart. You say what you need to say, and I'll listen."

She let out a deep sigh. "Where do I begin? My name isn't

Catherine Archer. At least, not anymore. When my stepfather adopted my sister and me, we changed it. To Stavros."

"The Greek Billionaire."

She nodded. "He's a wolf shifter. Alpha of the Lykos Pack." She paused. "I was seven when my biological father died and left us penniless. My mother didn't have a choice; she accepted a position as a tutor to Aristotle Stavros' three sons. He and his wife had recently divorced, and he wanted someone to look after his children since he traveled a lot on business. He wanted a female tutor, someone who could teach them manners and graces. Of course, my sister and I came to live on Lykos as well. That's the island where the pack lives."

"How did he come to adopt you, then?"

"Well, the short story is Ari fell in love with Mama. She was his mate, as it turned out. His first marriage was an arranged one, to build an alliance and produce strong children." She bit her lip. "For a while, we were happy. Ari adopted us, and we started calling him Papa. I had three older stepbrothers who I adored. And then Mama got pregnant. She had a baby girl." Her throat closed, and the tears began to form in her eyes. Matthew slipped his hand into hers and squeezed it.

"You don't have to—"

She shook her head. "No, I need to tell you the rest. So you'll understand. When it was time to have the baby, Mama wanted her born in England. They fought about it, but he eventually relented. He loved her that much. So our youngest, Cordelia, was born in an English hospital." The stench of the antiseptic seemed to burn her nostrils, but she continued. "After giving birth, Mama grew weaker. The doctors didn't know why she wasn't recovering; it had been a normal birth." The memories came flooding back. Of that sterile, dull hospital. Of watching Mama wither away. "It turned out some anti-shifter group found out Mama had given birth to a wolf pup. They got one of their own inside the hospital and were slowly poisoning her and Cordelia. Cordy was a shifter; she recovered. But Mama..."

She didn't even realize it, but she was sobbing now. Matthew drew her into his arms and let her cry.

"Then what happened?"

Catherine swallowed audibly. "Papa ... he went insane with grief. Took me, Christina, and Cordy back to Lykos. Shut himself and us away from the world. He wasn't going to let anyone harm us. We didn't leave for years. We had private tutors, doctors, anything and everything we needed, flown into the island. Lykos became a mini-city and we had every luxury you could think of, although for a while it was more like a prison." Her voice was bitter now. "Papa never would have let us leave if we didn't convince him that Mama would have wanted us to go to boarding school and university in England. She'd been a teacher, after all. So, he let me and Christina go to London." She smiled. "Christina hated it. She had fully embraced being part of the Lykos Pack, even though she was human. After she finished her degree, she went right back to work for Stavros International. I *loved* London. Loved the entire scene. I loved the freedom. I wanted to stay. I found a job I liked and this amazing apartment in SoHo for cheap."

"So why did you run away?"

"Well, the job that I enjoyed and paid well? Papa had cashed in some favors to get it for me. Even had some of his guys working in the office to watch me. That great deal on that apartment? He'd been paying a significant portion of the rent. And he had bought the apartment across from mine, so he could put a security detail on me 24/7. My entire life was a lie, another prison Ari Stavros constructed."

"What did you do?"

"I confronted him, of course. I was furious and told him I was going to go somewhere he couldn't get to me. I'd make it on my own. He wanted me back on Lykos. He …" Her voice faltered. "He threatened to marry me off to one of his lieutenants. So I would stay."

Matthew's silvery eyes glowed. "He *what?*"

"He said that I would learn to love my husband in time, and if not, my children for sure. So, I ran away." She turned away from him and looked out the window. "I went to Los Angeles. I was happy for a time, until … I … I swear Matthew, I didn't kill anyone."

"I know," he said. He moved to the other side of the bed to face her. "What happened in L.A.?"

"My roommate, Rissa, she'd gotten involved with one of the Chesnovak Brotherhood Pride, the local Russian shifter mob. One day, I came home and they were there and Rissa was dead." The tears came back, and she wiped them with the back of her hand. "I thought about going back to Lykos. The pack would protect me. But at what price? So I ran again. And I arrived here. I'm so sorry, Matthew. I'm sorry for bringing all this on you and your town. I put everyone in danger just by being here, knowing the Pride was after me."

He let out a huff. "As if I couldn't protect you from one measly lion pride."

"I know, but … that's not on you. I did my best to stay away from you. To protect you and to protect my heart. I didn't want to be trapped in a gilded cage again."

"I would never trap you," he said softly. "I would do

anything for you. I'm sorry I hesitated that day when Meacham came."

"What? You tried to protect me. But I couldn't watch them take you down. Matthew, I ..." She took a deep breath. "I love you too much. "

His eyes grew wide. "Catherine ..." As gently as he could, he gathered her into his arms and kissed her. "I love you, too."

"You do?" she asked.

"Of course. I've known it from the beginning. You're my mate."

"I was scared when you told me that. I'd seen what it did to Papa when he lost Mama. But ..." She stopped suddenly, a warmth spreading through her. Like warm waves of water soothing her. It was like the load she'd been carrying around for months had been lifted from her shoulders. She couldn't explain it. It was something she hadn't felt before, but it felt ... right. "Matthew? What happened?"

"I think ... that's the mating bond," he said, his eyes were wide with surprise, then turned warm with love. "Dad always told me ... I would know it when it came."

"It is true then. I'm your mate."

He nodded. "And I'm yours. And I promise you'll be safe from now on. I'll protect you forever, and I won't let them take you away from me."

"Oh, Matthew ..." She frowned. "Wait, what do you mean take me away?"

"Oh right," he said in a sheepish tone. "About that." Matthew filled her in on what had happened when Christina arrived.

Catherine slapped herself on the forehead. "I forgot about the last message I had sent her. I didn't check in with her. She must have gotten worried. Christina is the only person who knew where I was." She may have been loyal to the pack, but they were still sisters, and Christina swore she would not tell Ari, her brothers, or even Cordy her whereabouts. "Shit. Christina's er … she's like a rabid dog that won't let go once she sets her mind on something."

"Tell me about it," he said wryly. "But don't worry, Jason's taking care of her."

"Your brother?" she asked with a raised brow.

"Yeah, she'll be fine," he said. "Trust me."

"It's not my sister I'm worried about."

CHAPTER 17

THEY SPOKE for a few minutes until Catherine declared she was tired. Matthew urged her to rest, so she closed her eyes and lay back on the bed. She was asleep in minutes.

The slamming of the door jolted her out of her dreamless sleep.

"What did you do to my sister?" Christina stormed in, her stiletto heels clicking angrily on the tile floor. She stomped over to Matthew, who was sitting in the armchair next to the bed. "You!" she hissed. "What are you doing in here? And what happened to Cristos? He was supposed to be watching the door until I got here."

"Christina!" Catherine admonished.

"I—Catherine?" She whipped around. "You're awake!" Christina scrambled over to her side and drew her into a hug. "I—sorry!" She let go when Catherine winced. "But ... how are you feeling? Are you recovered? When did you wake up?"

Catherine looked at her sister's worried face, and she felt her mouth widen into a smile involuntarily. Had it been a year since she'd seen her twin? They'd never been separated for so long;

they'd even shared a womb, after all. If she was honest with herself, not seeing Christina had been the worst part of her exile. "I've missed you so much, Chrissy," she said, her voice shaking.

Christina's jaw dropped, and her eyes were shiny with tears. "I've missed you, too." They embraced again, and when they pulled away, both their cheeks were wet. "I'm here to take you home. I—"

"No," Matthew growled from behind them. "She's not going anywhere."

"She's *my* sister," Christina said. "I have every right to take her home."

"And I'm her *mate*."

Christina's eyes grew as large as saucers. "Catherine? Is this true? Are you mated to this dragon?"

"Yes," she answered, looking at Matthew with warm eyes. "I am."

Christina brows drew together in confusion. "I don't understand."

"I love him, Christina," she said. "Don't you believe me?"

"I do," she answered with a shrug. "I just didn't think … I thought you wanted to get away from shifters and that life."

Catherine laughed. "Believe me; I know the irony." She reached out and took her sister's hand. "But it just happened. Call it fate, something that brought me to this place and to my mate. I'm staying in Blackstone."

"Go ahead and tell your father," Matthew added. "I will fight him with every last bone in my body if I have to."

"Papa would never …" She turned to Catherine. "He's changed. I swear to you. He said those things to you in anger. But he realized he was wrong, and he's been trying to make amends."

"Does he know where I am? That I went to L.A.?"

Christina shook her head. "I didn't tell him anything, but I think he suspected I knew. He didn't try to pry it out of me, though. He loves you and misses you. And he doesn't want to marry you off."

"How can I be sure?" Catherine asked.

"You can ask him yourself," a low, masculine voice said.

Catherine's head turned to the doorway. "P-P-Papa?"

Aristotle Stavros' imposing figure filled the doorway. He was just as she'd remembered—tall and dark, though his hair had turned silvery white over the years. His face, though weathered, was still handsome, and it was easy to understand how her Mama had fallen in love with him. However, there was something in his eyes that seemed tired.

"*Katerina*," he said softly as he walked toward her. "I … I'm so happy to see you are alive."

"I had to tell him," Christina said. "I'm sorry. I thought you were dying. I snuck off with the jet, and when he called me, I had to let him know."

"I'm sorry, Katerina," Ari said. "For pushing you away. I wasn't going to marry you off like chattel. You are my daughter."

"Papa …" Tears burned behind her eyes. The memories— the good ones—came back. Like when he taught her and Christina how to swim in the brilliant blue Mediterranean Sea. Or when she broke her leg playing on the craggy rocks behind their villa, and he heard her cries, found her, then carried her all the way back inside. This man had loved her mother so much, had loved her and Christina, even though they weren't his biological children. "I missed you. But I'm not sorry I ran away."

His head hung low. "It seems the more I try to hold on to something I love, the more it wants to get away."

"I just wanted to be normal and free, Papa," she said. "I didn't want to be free of *you*." She opened her arms, and he eagerly accepted her embrace.

"Papa has been trying to make amends," Christina added. "He even let Cordelia leave Lykos. She's in a boarding school in England, just like Mama wanted."

"She is?" Catherine asked.

Ari nodded. "I miss her so, but she's loving it there. We talk every day. It's a special boarding school for shifters."

"She's getting to be very proficient in languages," Christina said proudly. "She already spoke Greek, English, French, and German when she enrolled, but she's taking extra classes in Japanese and Italian this year."

"Wow, I can't believe ..." She was happy for Cordy. She was a bright child, though very sheltered. And she missed her youngest sister so much.

Ari turned to Matthew, his expression serious. "So, you are my daughter's mate."

"I am," Matthew answered. His silvery eyes remained hard. "She will stay here, and I will protect her forever. If she chooses."

Catherine gave him a warm smile. "Of course, I choose you."

Ari's face turned crestfallen, but he managed a sad smile. "I was hoping to have my little girl back, but I suppose I can't stop fate."

"Papa," Catherine said, placing an arm on his hand. "I'll always be your daughter."

"I know, but ..." He turned back to Matthew. "Blackstone

Dragon, I entrust you with one of my greatest treasures. I implore you to keep her safe and *happy*."

"I will, Alpha," he said with a nod. "Thank you for your trust and your treasure."

"Hey, Matthew, you seal the deal yet?"

Matthew, Catherine, Christina, and Ari's heads all turned to the doorway as Jason casually strolled into the room, hands in his pockets.

"*You*." Christina's eyes turned into narrow slits. "What are you doing here? I told you I never wanted to see you again."

"Aww, babe, are you still embarrassed about this morning?" Jason asked with a cheeky grin. "I told you, a little drool between friends is nothing to be worried about."

Christina's face turned red. "I am *not* your friend."

Catherine frowned. "What the hell happened?"

Her twin's hands rolled into fists at her side. "This ... *vlaca* ... came to my hotel and pretended to be my driver. I told him I wanted to come to the hospital, then he got us lost." She let out a frustrated cry. "And then ... his truck stalled and we were stuck all night on the side of the road. In the cold."

Jason snorted. "It was for a good cause. All's well that ends well and all that shit, right?"

Catherine laughed. "Jason Lennox pretended to be a driver?"

"He ... Jason Lennox?" Christina looked at Jason and then at Matthew and narrowed her eyes. "Are you distant cousins or something?"

Matthew's eyes grew wide, and Jason began shaking his head, drawing his fingers across his neck in a slicing motion.

They sure were acting weird, Catherine thought. "Yeah, they're twins," Catherine explained. "At least that's what they keep telling me." She still couldn't understand how anyone would mistake Matthew and Jason for twins.

"Twins?" Christina said. "But they look nothing … hold on." She stomped over to Jason and poked a finger in his chest. "If you're brothers, that means you're a dragon, too."

"Uh-huh."

"*Asshole!*" She swatted him in the chest. "You could have built a fire. Hell, you could have flown us back here!"

"I could have," Jason said, wrapping a hand around her wrist and gently pulling it away. "But where's the fun in that?"

"Arrgghhhh! I'm going to call Cordelia and our brothers," she said as she marched out of the room.

"Excuse me," Ari said as he nodded to Matthew and Catherine. "I should go check on my daughter. She's got a nasty temper." Ari hugged Catherine, promising that he was going to stay a few days, and then shook hands with Matthew before he left.

She turned to Matthew. "What's going on?"

He had a big grin on his face, which was directed at Jason. "Did I ever tell you this saying my mother had about twins in her family?"

She narrowed her eyes. "I don't think so."

"Right. Well—"

"Don't," Jason said, his eyes going stormy. "Please don't."

Matthew laughed and continued anyway. "According to the legend, 'the one who knows you from your twin is your soulmate.' We never knew what that meant until you came and could clearly tell us apart."

"What?" Catherine said, her voice raising. "So … you really *are* identical twins? Everyone else thinks you look alike?"

Matthew nodded. "Everyone except you. And, now, your sister."

Catherine's jaw dropped. "Does that mean …"

"It's a stupid legend," Jason said with a growl. "I'm sure it's because *you two* are twins. You share the same DNA, so she can see what you see, too. That's all."

"My dragon knows Christina isn't my mate, though," Matthew added. "What does yours say?"

Jason kicked one of the chairs in the corner. "Whatever. Glad you guys sorted it out. I'm out of here." He gave them a wave goodbye and left the room.

Matthew watched his twin's retreating back. "Hmmm, well this is definitely interesting."

"Christina and Jason?" She shook her head. "I can't think of two people more ill-suited for each other."

"Well, I didn't ever think I would find a mate," Matthew said, drawing her close to his side. "But here I am."

Catherine laughed. "Yes, and here *I* am." She looked up at him, her heart threatening to burst out of her chest with happiness. "And here I'll stay."

EPILOGUE

MATTHEW PULLED into the last empty spot in the lot outside The Den and cut the engine. "Are you okay?"

Catherine rolled her eyes. "I told you, I'm fine." She leaned over and kissed him. "In fact, I'm so fine I think we should go back home again and I can show you how *fine* I am." She wiggled her eyebrows at him.

He tossed his head back and laughed. "As much fun as that sounds, it would be rude to just blow everyone off. We should head inside, at least pop in for one drink."

"I don't even know why we're here," she grumbled. "Can't I meet Amelia tomorrow? I'm sure Ben's sister is a lovely girl, but I want to celebrate some more." She lifted her hand, the five-carat diamond sparkling even in the low light of the car. Her smile was as wide as the Golden Gate Bridge.

"We can celebrate again tonight," he said as he pulled her in for a quick kiss. "Ben will be disappointed if we're not all here."

Catherine pouted. Ben was too much of a nice guy, and

she would hate to be rude to him and his sister. "Fine. But I'm getting some more tonight."

"You can have as much as you want," he said. "For the rest of your life."

Dr. Parry let Catherine out of the hospital a few days early, but only if she had proper care at home and didn't strain herself. Matthew hired a round-the-clock nurse to help her out as she recovered, plus he took care of her when he got home. She discretely asked the doctor when she would be clear for *physical activities* and the doctor answered that it would be in two weeks. Which was today. The doctor himself came over to the castle this morning to check her wounds, which were healed nicely.

She was hoping to have some alone time with him finally. Meg had set up a romantic meal in the library, and as soon as they were done, he got down on one knee and proposed to her. She said yes, of course, then proceeded to rip his clothes off and have her way with him. He joked that she was more excited about having sex than his proposal.

Matthew helped her out of the car, and they walked hand-in-hand into the Den.

"Surprise!" Cheers, shouts, and hoots greeted them as they entered the bar. There were even confetti guns and poppers.

"What is going on?" Catherine shouted as she looked around. There was a big, hand-painted sign over the bar that said "Congratulations Matthew and Catherine."

"Surprise, sweetheart," he said, kissing her. "Everyone wanted to celebrate with us."

People came up to them, hugging them and giving their congratulations as they walked by. When they got to their table, Jason, Nate, Kate, Sybil, and a young woman who was probably Amelia, were already waiting for them.

"Congratulations! Oh my God, I'm so happy!" Sybil said as she pulled Catherine into a big hug.

"What would you have done if she had said no?" Kate asked, as she threw back a shot of whiskey.

"She wouldn't have said no," Matthew said.

Catherine laughed. "Well, I might have, if you hadn't finally given up your virtue," she said with a wry smile, which had Nate and Jason jeering.

"Hey, it was the doctor's orders," he said, throwing his hands up.

"I'm Amelia," the tall woman with dark blond hair and green eyes said, extending her hand. "Ben's sister."

"Nice to meet you," Catherine said. "Where is Ben?"

"He's been delayed, but he'll be here soon."

As if on cue, the door slammed open, and Ben's large frame filled the doorway. He gave them a big smile, then waved and lumbered over to them. It seemed he was so distracted that he didn't notice the petite waitress in his path. He bumped into her and she toddled back. Without looking down, he grabbed her by the shoulders to steady her, then simply lifted her up and placed her out of his way as he continued to amble toward them. The young woman let out a squeak and stared after him, but Ben didn't even look back.

"Sorry," Ben apologized as he got to the table. "Had to do some overtime today." He hugged his sister and welcomed her home. "I ..." His face turned blank, and he turned around.

"You okay, buddy?" Matthew asked. "You look like you've seen a ghost."

Ben shook his head and ran a hand down his face. "No ... I thought I heard ... And then I smelled ..." He shrugged his shoulders. "Never mind." He looked at Catherine. "So, congratulations, guys! And welcome to the family." He gathered her into a fierce hug. "Glad to know this grumpy dragon ain't gonna be working himself to death or brooding alone in his castle anymore."

Catherine laughed. "I've given him a monthly limit on the brooding."

"So, did you set a date yet?" Sybil asked. "I know you've only been engaged a couple of hours. But Mom and Dad want to know so they can come home for the wedding."

Catherine had met Hank and Riva over video call a few times, and though they were eager to meet her, she insisted they could continue their trip. They could all figure out a later time to get together, since she was still recovering from her wounds. "We're thinking the end of the month."

"That soon?" Kate narrowed her eyes and placed a hand on Catherine's tummy. "You got a bun baking in there?"

"Kate," Sybil admonished.

Catherine looked up at Matthew shyly. A baby with her mate? She thought about holding a small, tiny person that was half her and half him. The thought warmed her heart. Judging by the look on his face, he was thinking the same thing, too.

"No." He shook his head, then added, "Not *yet*."

"But we're decided there's no need to wait to get married," Catherine said. "We're not doing anything fancy, and that should be enough time to get my family here, and Cordy will be out of school. Christina will be here earlier to help me plan."

Jason's eyes darkened at the mention of her sister's name. He took a shot of tequila, then another, and slammed both glasses on the table. "Say, Nate, those ladies look lonely." He nodded to a group of girls at another table. "Why don't we go keep them company?"

"You sure you're not going to strike out again?" Nate asked. "Because you know last time—"

"Shut up," Jason growled and threw back another shot. "Later," he said as he walked over to the women. Nate shrugged and followed his friend.

"What crawled up his ass?" Kate asked.

Catherine looked at Matthew, and he shrugged. Since that day at the hospital, neither of them had brought up the incident. Did she believe in the legend? She wasn't sure, but then again no one else she talked to said they looked different. Not Sybil. Not Meg nor Christopher. Not even their parents. Riva said she could tell them apart by their mannerisms, but to her, they looked exactly the same. But maybe, like Jason said, it was because she and Christina were twins. He never talked about her, and whenever anyone uttered the word mate, he would bristle and change the subject or walk away.

Christina never mentioned Jason either, nor what had transpired between them that night. She had been speaking with her twin sister regularly, and though Christina had her reservations about Matthew, she was happy when Catherine had told her about the engagement today. It would take a lot of work to switch her schedule, but Christina promised to come at least a week before the wedding. She also confided in her about what she'd been *really* doing at Stavros International for the past year. While Catherine wasn't thrilled, it had confirmed to her Papa had indeed changed.

"You seem far away," Matthew said as he leaned closer. "Regretting saying yes already?"

"Ha!" she crowed. "You're not getting out of marrying me that easily."

"I thought I would be the one dealing with a runaway bride," he said wryly.

"Oh no, no more running away," she said. "I'm home." Blackstone was her home. Matthew was her home. For now and always.

The End

Thanks for reading! Want to read some bonus and extra scenes from this book, including some sexy scenes that are too hot to publish? Sign up for my newsletter here: http://aliciamontgomeryauthor.com/mailing-list/

You'll get access to ALL the bonus materials from all my books, two FREE contemporary novels and my **FREE** novella **The Last Blackstone Dragon,** featuring the love story of Matthew's parents, Hank and Riva.

Thank you so much for coming on this journey to the Blackstone Mountains with me! And, as you can tell, it's only just begun, so I hope you stick around.

Some of you may be wondering why I wrote this story, especially since, if you've read my True Mates series, I have a ton more storylines and books to write for that one. Well, I realized at some point this year (maybe around the time I was writing All for Connor), I was suffering a bit of a burnout from the True Mates world. I really wanted to continue the stories and begin generation two, but I was running out of fresh ideas. I needed a break, and so I wrote The Last Blackstone Dragon.

The idea for The Last Blackstone Dragon came from the old robber barons of the industrial age. I was fascinated with the stories of these tycoons, like John Jacob Astor, John D. Rockefeller, Andrew Carnegie, etc. So, I thought, what if I used the same idea but with shifters? And so Blackstone was born. I wrote Riva and Hank's story (Hank was originally going to Matthew and Jason's older brother) and spawned a whole new world of shifters.

I hope you enjoyed reading The Blackstone Dragon Heir and that you're looking forward to the next book in the Blackstone series! I want to hear what you think, so email me at alicia@aliciamontgomeryauthor.com for your thoughts or all other comments. I also hope that you leave me a review, as reviews are what keeps authors like me going and writing. And if you didn't like it - that's okay, I'd still love to hear from you.

All the best,

Alicia

PREVIEW: THE BLACKSTONE BAD DRAGON

Four Weeks Ago...

Pretending to be his twin brother was something Jason Lennox was very good at.

Even now, as he sat in his brother's office, no one had suspected he wasn't Matthew. Not the security guard who greeted him this morning as he entered the lobby. Not the people in the elevator who had given him nervous nods. Not even some of the long-time employees of Lennox Corp. People mixed him and Matthew up all the time, so acting like his cool, more aloof twin was just a matter of switching his personality.

No one could tell them apart, not even their parents or sister, though as they grew older and developed their own separate interests and personalities, people started to notice the difference. Matthew was inclined to stay in his room and finish his homework—even on a Friday night,—while he preferred the company of his friends. Matthew was more serious, which is why he was chosen to be CEO of Lennox Corporation when their mother retired. But he wasn't resentful or anything. He didn't want that responsibility. He preferred running the Lennox Foundation and working in the blackstone mines in his dragon form. His inner dragon loved nothing more than being free. And he couldn't do that if he was stuck in board meetings all day.

Still, despite their differing personalities, the two were as close as anyone could be. Jason would do anything for Matthew. Pretending to be him for the day to help save his twin's reputation and the family company was easy enough.

While he couldn't analyze spreadsheets and stock reports like his brother, he could get by for just a day. When the staff looked at him in his immaculate suit and tie, hair groomed back perfectly and a cool expression on his face, it was easy to fool them into believing he was Matthew. *Easiest gig in the world.*

The phone on the desk rang, and he quickly picked it up. "Matthew Lennox," Jason answered.

"It's me." *Matthew.*

"Oh good." The tension fell from his shoulders and put his feet up on the large oak desk. "What's happening? She's okay, right?"

And this was the reason he was pretending to be his twin. Matthew's mate, Catherine, had been injured following an attack by a pride of lions who had been trying to kill her. Matthew was able to save her in time, but she'd been badly hurt. He couldn't leave her side, which is why Jason had to stand in for him at work. He just hoped she would pull through because it would destroy Matthew if anything happened to her, plus, Jason happened to actually like Catherine. She was a good person.

"Yeah … she's stable," Matthew said.

"So, what's wrong?" Jason asked, sensing his twin's distress.

"Well, you see … it turns out Catherine has family. A sister. We met and things didn't go too well. She blames me for what happened and she's trying to take her away."

"Fuck, no!" Jason swiveled the leather chair around and got to his feet. "She can't do that. What do we gotta do to stop her?"

"That's why I called. She left the hospital to grab some things from her hotel room and is coming back soon. You have to delay her somehow."

"And how am I going to do that?"

"I don't know, just … pretend to be me. Intercept her at the lobby and tell her you're sorry about today and that you just want to talk to her. Charm her. Make her think like you're on her side and that you're not trying to stop her. We just need some time to get into Catherine's room so I can talk to her."

"Ah," Jason said with a nod. "Gotcha."

"Oh and by the way—shit!" Matthew cursed. "Sorry, Jason, I gotta go."

And so an hour and a half later, he arrived at the lobby of The Ritz Ski Resort, just thirty miles out of Blackstone town. He sat in one of the wingback chairs, nursing a whiskey as he scanned the area for … what was her name? Christina. Matthew had forgotten to tell him what this Christina looked like. He supposed if she was related to Catherine, they would look alike. Would she be pretty? Jason let out a snort. Who cares? If she was trying to take Catherine away, then Jason would do whatever it took to stop her. Even if she looked like the Wicked Witch of the West, he would do his best to charm her, at the very least, distract her long enough for Matthew to convince Catherine they were mates and make her stay with him forever.

He let out another snort and swirled the crystal glass in his hand before taking another sip. Not that he wasn't happy for his twin. Matthew was finally getting that stick out of his ass, and that was all thanks to Catherine. Dragons rarely found mates, after all. Matthew's dragon not only recognized Catherine as his mate, but also confirmed a legend from their mom's side of the family.

Their mother, Riva, told them of a saying from the Sinclair family: the one who knows you from your twin is your soul mate. And it seemed Matthew had indeed found his. Jason wouldn't have believed it if he hadn't seen it himself. Despite seeing them side-by-side, Catherine didn't believe they were twins. In fact, she said they looked different in her eyes. Jason had found her cute, even flirted with her, but backed off quickly when it became obvious Matthew's dragon had already staked its claim.

Good for him. Having a mate was something his brother needed. Someone to lean on during the tough times, and of course, have cute little dragonlings who would carry on the family name. If he had to name one reason to be glad about not being the heir to Lennox Corp., it would be that he was free. Free to do whatever he wanted. And whomever he wanted. In fact—he was antsy now. He hoped this wouldn't take too long, because all he wanted was to head over to The Den and find some friendly company for the evening. Someone new and exciting. There was nothing like the thrill of the chase, the feel of a gorgeous woman in his bed. And—

The glass in his hand dropped with a soft thud, spilling the amber contents onto plush, white carpet. But he didn't notice it; in fact, the entire room seemed to quiet down as he stared ahead. His heart began to hammer against his rib cage.

She walked into the lobby of The Ritz like she was a queen, like she owned it. Dressed in a white wool coat, stiletto heels, and wearing a cool expression on her beautiful face. A very familiar face.

"Goddamn Matthew." His brother had conveniently forgotten to mention something of importance. Christina wasn't just Catherine's sister. She was her *twin*. But even though they were the spitting image of each other, there was something about her that was different and he couldn't stop staring. She turned her head and ice-blue eyes stared right back at him and in that moment, his heart stopped beating. Everything slowed down and froze.

Mine.

Huh? Jason shook his head.

It was suddenly noisy in the lobby again and time went back to normal speed. But she was still staring at him, and for just a brief second he saw that cool mask disappear. She had seemed surprised to see him, flustered even. *Of course she was,* he told himself. She and Matthew had met earlier and had a nasty confrontation. As her cool demeanor returned, she turned away and began to walk toward the doors.

Shit! Can't let her get away! Jason shot to his feet, threw a couple of bills on the table, and strode after Christina. She was standing by the door, hands on her hips, an impatient look on her face.

"Uhm, Christina," he called as he stopped in front of her. "I'm glad I caught up with you."

She looked up at him, those light-blue eyes pinning him with a frosty gaze. "Excuse me?"

"Look, I came here to apologize. For this morning?" God, he sounded like an idiot. He really should have gotten more details from Matthew.

"What are you talking about? Do I know you?" she asked with a frown. Her accent was posh and elegant, very different from her sister's.

Was this chick on something? "We met this morning and—"

"You must have mistaken me for someone else," she said, then looked away impatiently.

"Wait, you don't know me?" he asked.

She turned back toward him, her gaze perusing him from head to toe. "I don't think so."

Oh no.

Oh hell *no.*

Jason's heart sped up again. *There's got to be some mistake.* "Listen, Christina. I—"

"Please don't address me in such a familiar tone," she snapped. "I told you, I'm not who you think I am."

"Christina...Archer?"

Her eyes narrowed to slits. "It's Stavros," she corrected. "So, obviously, I'm not who you're looking for." She began to walk away from him and headed out the front door.

Mine.

"Shut the fuck up!" he growled at his inner dragon. No, there was some mistake. Christina whatever her name was, was *not* his mate. He didn't want a mate. He didn't *need* a mate. His life was perfectly fine the way it was. Drinking and having fun, and fucking any woman he wanted. "Shit!" As much as he wanted to run in the opposite direction, he'd promised Matthew he would keep her away from the hospital.

As he walked out of the hotel lobby, he told himself there had to be a reasonable explanation. Christina and Catherine shared DNA. *Yeah, that was it.* It didn't mean Christina was his mate. It couldn't, because otherwise, karma was really kicking his ass.

The frigid night air hit his face, but he shrugged it off. He was a shifter, after all, and his own dragon fire could melt all the snow on the mountains. Glancing around, he saw Christina huddled under a heat lamp, arms around herself, and her head glancing up and down the driveway of The Ritz. Shoving his hands into his pockets, he walked over to her.

"Are you following me?" she asked.

"Look, if you'd just let me explain—"

"I told you ... Wait." Her eyes lit up in recognition. "I think I know who you are."

A spark of hope lit up in Jason, and he ignored his dragon's protests.

"You're the new driver that the car company sent," she said. "The dispatcher said she'd be sending someone new, since my driver was called away."

"Yeah?" *Driver?*

The expression on her face turned from anger to relief. "Oh, that must be it." She frowned. "I wish you'd identified yourself sooner. Don't you have ID or something?"

"I ... lost it," he said. Okay, so she thought he was a limo driver. He'd take that. After all, mate or not (and definitely not), he had a job to do. He couldn't let Matthew down. "Uhm, so yeah, where'd you want to go?"

"To Blackstone Hospital," she said, placing her hands on her hips. "Well?"

He didn't realize he'd been staring at her. How could he not? Standing this close to her, he could see how smooth and like porcelain her skin was. Her cheeks were pink from the heat of the lamp and her blue eyes shone like crystal. There was just something about her that made him want to stare for hours.

"Right," he cleared his throat. "I'll get the car."

Jason walked across the parking lot, then climbed into his jacked up Chevy Silverado. Shit, if he knew he'd be playing chauffeur, he would have taken one of the company cars. At least his truck looked shiny and new. Not exactly something a limo company would have, but he'd just have to come up with some excuse.

He maneuvered the truck to the driveway, slipped out, and walked around to open the door for Christina.

"*This* is the car?" she asked, raising a delicate brow.

He nodded toward the road, which was icy and covered in snow. "That's why they sent me," he said. *Good save.* "Look lady, if you want a fancy limo or something, you can wait until morning. But in these conditions, you'll need my truck."

She hesitated for a moment. "Fine." She climbed up, though the truck was so high, it was a feat in her skinny stilettos and tight skirt suit, though she managed it with grace. Jason tried not to stare at the perfectly-formed ass as she got inside. With a cheeky grin and a tip of an imaginary hat, he closed the door and walked over to the driver's side.

Okay, gotta think about how to keep her away, Jason thought as he slipped back into the vehicle. He glanced at the rearview mirror. Christina was staring outside, her face drawn into a worried expression. Of course she was anxious. Her twin sister had been shot and fighting for her life. If that had happened to Matthew, he'd be worried too. He wished he could reach out and smooth that wrinkle between her eyebrows.

"*Ahem.*" Christina was staring back at him.

"Right," he said, regaining his composure. "Let's go."

"So," he began. "Why'd you choose to stay here if you needed to go to the hospital? Seems so far away."

She let out an impatient sigh. "My assistant made the reservation. She said that with the tourist season in Blackstone, all the hotels in the area were booked up."

"Ah, I see. And why'd you come all the way to Blackstone?"

"It's a private matter," she replied. "And I'd prefer to keep it that way." She looked away, crossing her arms, and looked out the window.

"Sorry," he murmured. There was no way this cold, stuck-up human was his mate, unless fate really did hate him. *Okay, no more small talk.* But, he needed a plan.

An idea popped into his head. She wasn't going to like it, but she probably wasn't going to like anything he came up with.

He continued along the main highway down the mountain. It was late enough that it was practically deserted. No other car had passed their way. Thanks to his shifter sight, he spotted a smaller road in the distance veering off gently. He made the detour, glancing up at the rearview mirror, but Christina stared down at her phone, fingers tapping on the screen rapidly. With a frustrated sigh, she put the phone back into her purse.

"Everything okay?" he asked.

"Yes. I mean, no." She shook her head. "I just lost reception on my phone. I was replying to my father. Anyway..." She frowned and looked around. "I don't recall leaving the main road when we drove up here before."

"It's a shortcut," he said. "Don't worry about it."

He drove for a couple of minutes, hoping the road wouldn't end soon. The problem was these types of mountain roads usually ventured off into private property or a dead-end. Either way, they would have to turn back. He needed another excuse to stall.

Then, inspiration hit him. He began to ease his foot off the gas, allowed the car slow to a stop then turned the ignition off.

"Uh-oh," he feigned.

"Uh-oh?" Christina said. "What do you mean, *uh-oh?*"

"Well, this hasn't happened in a long while." He pretended to turn the key in the ignition several times.

"What's going on?" she asked, her voice rising.

"It's nothing, don't worry," he reassured her, opening the door and sliding out.

"Don't worry? I—"

He shut the door before she could protest further. She *really* wasn't going to like this.

Jason walked to the front of the truck and lifted up the hood. Christina couldn't see him, so he stood there, pretending to look into the engine and trying to come up with some excuse. Finally, he put the hood down and hopped back into the truck.

"Well?" Christina asked, her eyes narrowed at him.

He shook his head. "The engine's shot."

"What do you mean? It was just fine a while ago."

"Yeah, well, cars are funny like that," he said, mentally crossing his fingers and hoping she didn't know shit about engines. "Must be the cold weather. Wasn't expecting it and the, uh, driver before me didn't fill up the antifreeze."

"Well, what are you going to do about it?" she asked. "Did you call your dispatcher? Your boss?"

"Yeah, about that…" He held up his phone. "No reception either. You have any luck with yours?"

Christina grabbed her phone from her purse and tapped on the screen. "Ugh. No."

"Well then," he said, settling into the seat. "I guess we'll have to wait."

"Excuse me? Wait here?" He could practically see the steam coming out from her ears. If she wasn't human, she would have made a great dragon. "We're in the middle of nowhere! Shouldn't we get help?"

"Lady, it's freezing out there." He pointed to her stilettos. "Are you going to be walking around dark mountain roads in those?"

"I...I..." Her face turned red. "Then what are *you* going to do?"

"You think I'm going out there?" he looked back at her incredulously and shook his head. "We'll stay here. When my dispatcher doesn't hear from us in an hour or two, she'll send someone to check. Don't worry," he reassured her. "This happens occasionally. We have systems in place for every eventuality." He reclined the seat, closed his eyes, and relaxed. "We just have to wait it out."

He heard her make an irritated huffing sound, then a resigned sigh. She shuffled around and when he turned to glance back at her, she had settled against the corner of the backseat, her coat draped over her, and legs tucked underneath. For a moment, Jason felt a surge of desire, watching her beautiful, peaceful face. He ignored it and closed his eyes.

Jason woke up later, jolted from sleep by the sound of something...chattering? Jason sat up, rubbed his eyes, and looked back.

Christina was lying down on the backseat. Her wool coat was draped over her like a blanket, but it was too short. Even curled up, her legs stuck out. The temperature must have dropped significantly in the last three hours, but he didn't notice because his shifter biology kept him warm.

His dragon roared in anger. *Damn animal.* Still, an ache pressed into his gut, seeing her cold and knowing it was his fault. She could get sick, if she wasn't already. *Fuck*, he cursed inwardly. Without thinking, he slipped out the driver's side and climbed into the backseat.

Jason nudged her over then draped her legs over his lap. "Jesus," he muttered. Her shapely legs were ice-cold. He glanced at her face to check on her, but she didn't wake up. In fact, she let out a sigh and moved lower, pressing her ass against his sides and curling her legs over his lap, seeking his warmth. He let out a groan as his cock stood at attention and adjusted his pants. He had to ignore the desire clawing at him because there was no way he was going to give in to it.

Available now on Amazon!

Made in United States
Orlando, FL
13 December 2021

11624667R00125